CAPONE'S KEYS

SALLY J. LING

Flamingo
Press

Capone's Keys

To contact the author, you may email her at:
info@sallyjling.com

Capone's Keys is a work of fiction. Names, characters, locations, and incidents are either the product of the author's imagination or are used fictitiously.

Cover designed by Andy Massari.

ISBN: 978-1-7371329-5-0

ACKNOWLEDGEMENTS

My sincere thanks to editor Kara Leigh Miller, and select individuals who assisted in the editing process by reading *Capone's Keys*.

TABLE OF CONTENTS

CAPONE'S KEYS

Chapter 1

Deerfield Beach, Florida
June 1948

"*D*on't forget your lunch." *Derick's mom, Maggie, leaned against the back door threshold and dangled the paper sack in her hand. Inside were a bologna sandwich, apple, and pretzels—lunch he would need as he launched himself, once again, on his great quest.*

"Be right there," Derick called, gazing up from the boat tethered at the dock.

In his frantic attempt to pack his gear into the boat—buckets, shovel, blanket, water—and concentrate on his mission, he had forgotten all about making lunch. In a few hours, his stomach would rumble loudly, desperate for food. Thank goodness for mothers.

Sally J. Ling

Derick's focus had been on getting to the peninsula and digging up the treasure. Not that he hadn't tried before. He'd taken dozens of trips up the Intracoastal to the acreage jutting off the mainland every time he got the treasure 'itch.' Today, for some reason, the 'itch' seemed more intense, his optimism more pronounced. Today, he would find the hidden booty.

He scrambled from the boat, ran up the walkway, and grabbed the bag from his mother's grasp. "Thanks, Mom," he said before rushing back to the boat.

He waved at his mother, then pulled the cord to start the motor on his Clinker-built wooden rowboat, oars drawn in. His father had fitted the bobbing craft with an Evenrude outboard motor to fight the strong Intracoastal current on both incoming and outgoing tides. It wasn't the sleekest vessel for the waterway, but it would do.

With the motor idling, Derick released the ropes from cleats on the dock, then motored out into the waterway, his brown hair plastered to his forehead by the wind. Large, puffy, white clouds littered the sky and mostly hid the sun, but the consequences of the sun's rays beat down upon him. Fortunately, he wore a short-sleeved shirt and brought along a wide-brimmed hat. They would help protect him; otherwise, his back, chest, and face would be burnt to a crisp by the time he returned home.

Derick headed north, knowing the parcel of land would be a challenge to get to as he faced the robust outgoing current and a headwind, but he was determined. He made it under the swing bridge at Hillsboro Blvd., waving to bridge tender Mr. William Belton Jones, known to locals as "Jonesy," and headed toward the peninsula. His favorite spot to come ashore was on the east side, where a small beach between the mangroves allowed him to pull the boat onto the sand.

Once he arrived, he opened his blanket and placed his supplies in it. Wrapping them up like a gift, he swung the pack over his shoulder, picked up the shovel, and hiked through the underbrush to a new spot on the north side of the property where he hadn't tried digging before.

After several hours of shoveling with nothing to show for his efforts except sand spurs and blisters, Derick heard a clunk. The sound wasn't the metal on metal he'd hoped for, but whatever he hit was solid, impenetrable, and not all sand like he was used to. He dropped to his knees and dug furiously with his bare hands. Out of breath and with sweat running in rivulets down his face, he encountered a gray canvas bag stained by the dark soil. Digging around the material, he freed the package from the dirt and lifted it from the hole with trembling hands. Setting the bundle on the soil, he carefully brushed the sand and dirt from its surface.

Derick was so excited to see what was inside that he had to stop himself from tearing the bag apart. Instead, he closed his eyes and took a deep breath, sending a prayer heavenward—

"Please let it be the treasure."

Tingling from head to toe, he pulled open the bag and peered inside.

"Yippee!" The loud whoop, meant for no one but himself, was quickly absorbed in the thick underbrush.

Inside the bag rested a rusted gray metal box. Derick pulled the container from the sack and shook it. The rattle of items inside was music to his ears. He desperately wanted to open the metal container, but it had a substantial lock on the clasp, so he quickly wrapped the container and his work items back up in his blanket, grabbed his shovel, and dashed back to the boat. When he got home, he'd take these things directly to his room.

Derick could guess until the cows came home what the box held, but until he snipped off the lock and opened the recovered prize, he'd never know. Yet, he believed beyond any shadow of a doubt that this was the treasure he'd been searching for, treasure buried over a dozen years ago on land rumored to have once been owned by the infamous Chicago gangster himself—Al Capone.

Chapter 2

Boca Raton, Florida

I jumped at the sound of the shrill train whistle as I sat on the patio with my next door neighbor Leslie enjoying a glass of lemonade. The piercing sound indicated someone at the front gate. I glanced at my phone only to see the face of an older woman appear on the security camera. She looked frazzled and unsteady—light brown, unkempt hair and darting grey eyes. I didn't recognize her.

"Yes, ma'am. Can I help you?"

She leaned toward the camera, her eyes glassy, unfocused. "Is this the Randi Brooks residence?" Her voice quivered as she spoke into the microphone.

"Yes," I said, unsure what to expect.

"I'm Sheila Eastway. I live in Deerfield Beach. I know this may sound strange, but I have something my late husband asked me to give you." Her face bobbed in front of the camera as she lifted a cardboard box to show me. "I think this is what got him killed." She hiccupped.

My eyes widened. "Killed?" I mouthed to Leslie.

She shooed me toward the front door with a wave of her hands.

"I'll be right there." I rose and opened the gate with a tap on my phone.

Too dumbfounded for either of us to speak, Leslie followed me to the entrance of Boca Grande, my home in the historic district of Old Floresta in Boca Raton, Florida. I opened the door to find Sheila Eastway pulling into the circular driveway. She appeared to be in her late seventies as the small, wiry woman dressed in baggy jeans and a white overblouse ambled toward the front door carrying a box.

"I'm sorry to interrupt you, especially on the weekend, but I wanted to give you this." Sheila shoved the taped cardboard container toward me. The odor of alcohol permeated the space between us.

"What is it?" I asked, accepting the box in bewilderment.

"I really don't know. My husband Derick died recently, but before he did, he told me if anything should happen to him, he wanted you to have this. I don't have a clue what's inside. He said you would figure it out." Sheila's words were delivered slowly, deliberately. She turned to go.

"Wait!" I called after her. "Why did he want *me* to have it?"

Shelia turned back. "He said he'd followed the local stories about your solving mysteries, and if anyone could make heads or tails out of this, you could. Oh, I almost forgot. Here's my name and phone number in case you want to get back in touch with me after you've had a chance to look at the contents." Sheila handed me a crumpled piece of paper.

I balanced the box while I stuffed the note into my pocket.

"Isn't there anything else you can tell me?" I asked.

"Perhaps, but Derick said you'd need to see what's inside first, and even then, a cursory look wouldn't help. You'd need to do some digging. He said I'd probably hear from you after that." Once again, Sheila turned to go, her gait wobbly.

"Well, where did he find what's inside the box?" I asked, desperate for more information.

Sheila looked around furtively, turned, and spoke in a low voice. "On Deerfield Island when he was eleven. Of course, the property wasn't known by that name then. Locals called the parcel Capone Island, named after the infamous gangster himself. I think what's inside this box is tied to my husband's death." Tears brimmed in Sheila's eyes.

"Have you spoken to the police? Showed them the box?"

"Derick said to give it directly to you. I'm honoring his wishes." She turned to walk back to her car.

"Please. Let me give you a ride home." I was unsure she should be driving.

"I made it here, didn't I?" Sheila got into her car and pulled out of the driveway without further explanation.

Leslie and I stood there stunned, hoping she'd make it home safely.

I carried the box into the kitchen and set the container on the island counter. Bigfoot, my polydactyl calico cat, jumped onto the stool beside me, his tail swishing and eyes peering inquisitively at the foreign object. As I opened the box, he caught a whiff of its odor and shot his nose up into the air. Then he vaulted from the stool just as Leslie and I pulled our heads back at the scent—a mixture of musty salt air with a hint of rotting seaweed. Taking a parting glance at Leslie and me, Bigfoot padded out the door. I guess 'curiosity killed the cat' wasn't what he had in mind this afternoon.

With our heads glued together, Leslie and I wore the curiosity of schoolgirls as we held our breaths and peered into the cardboard container at a gray rust-encrusted lockbox. My name, Randi Brooks, scribbled on a piece of paper and taped to the lid, stared back at us.

Letting out my breath, I lifted the lockbox from its cardboard container, withdrew a screwdriver from my catch-all drawer, and pried open the corroded latch. Leslie and I gasped in unison at what we saw inside—a slew of old safe deposit keys covered in light oxidation. Their presence made this unexpected bequest even more mysterious.

"Safe deposit keys got Derick Eastway killed?" asked Leslie.

"The safe deposit boxes must contain something very important."

"And deadly," added Leslie, eyeballing me.

We continued to gawk at the keys in silence. Sheila hadn't given us much information.

"Do you think the lockbox really belonged to Al Capone?" I asked. A rectangular paper tag discolored by yellowish-brown stains was attached to each key by an equally yellowish-brown string.

"I don't know, Tootsie." Leslie cocked her head to one side. "I do know Capone supposedly bought this little triangular piece of vacant land between Boca Raton and Deerfield Beach around 1930, right before his conviction for income tax evasion. The land is a park now called Deerfield Island Park. I haven't been there in years."

"Maybe we should visit the renowned island." I gazed at Leslie with great anticipation.

"I love the way you think." Her eyes sparkled with eagerness at the opportunity for us to take another road trip, even though the island was only a few miles away.

"About the keys, I don't think we should touch them. Let's put each one in a plastic baggie, and then we can examine them more carefully." I pulled a box of plastic sandwich bags from the drawer beside the refrigerator along with a pair of tongs. Leslie held the baggies open while I plucked each key and dropped the curious item into its bag.

Leslie selected one baggie after another and examined the tags. "They have writing on both sides, but some are so smudged or faded they're beyond reading."

"Maybe Connor can help us. Perhaps one of his forensic buddies can put them under a special light or manipulate the writing on a computer so we can read the lettering. Right now, though, let's concentrate on the ones we can decipher."

Connor, my husband of two months, was a former CID Special Agent for the Army for whom he still did contract work. CID Special Agents were like civilian crime scene investigators on steroids and equivalent to FBI or Secret Service agents—highly knowledgeable regarding the law and skilled in crime scene investigative methods. Connor helped me with advice and processing evidence on numerous occasions in my other sleuthing adventures, and just three months ago, he returned Raul Gonzales to the U.S. Not only was Raul a Mexican drug cartel member who ran drugs into South Florida, but he'd also murdered my parents by mistake.

The words on each key tag, at least the ones we could read, appeared to follow the same format—a bank's name on one side, a person's name on the other. Each had different handwriting that fit on the label.

"Do you recognize any of the bank names?" I asked Leslie. Since she was a third-generation Boca Raton resident and local historian, I figured if anyone was familiar with the names of old banks in the area, it would be her.

Leslie adjusted the hair clip that held her long gray hair away from her face. "Some seem familiar, but there have been many changes in the banking industry since our unidentified person put these keys in the box. Some banks went out of business when the Florida land boom and banking industry went bust in the mid-1920s. Others merged into the ones we know now. I think our best bet is to work backward. That will tell us how old the lockbox is so we can look for banks around that time. Get your laptop, Tootsie."

"Tootsie" was a nickname Leslie had given me when I was a child. She looked after me when school was out until my parents came home from working at A Stitch in Time, their fabric and upholstery shop. When Mom and Dad were unexpectedly murdered a year ago, I inherited the business at age thirty-three.

Using my former production talents and experience as a Capitol Hill news producer, I added a video production studio between the buildings and created a DIY channel for fabric crafts and upholstery projects. The project's goal was to increase exposure and revenues to the business and give a portion of our revenues back to the community through the nonprofit Greyhound Rescue and Rehabilitation. We accomplished both goals.

I rushed to the den and returned with my laptop to search for Derick Eastway's name in Find-a-Grave.

"Here he is." I pointed to the screen. "Derick Eastway died three months ago; he was eighty-three."

"That means he was a year older than I am when he died," said Leslie. "That puts him born in 1937 and eleven in 1948. So, we know the lockbox is at least seventy-two years old. But who knows how long the box was on the island before he found it?"

"True. Now, the fun begins."

"The fun?"

"Yes, what we do best—following the leads. Let's start with the keys."

I brought out my sizeable magnifying glass to see the writing on the key tags more clearly. As we went through each key, I wrote a number on a small stickie note and stuck the paper to each baggie. Creating a table, I typed the sticky note number along with the person's name, the bank, or what I could read of the words, and the safety deposit box number into each column. We could only make out the printing on both sides of five of the nineteen keys tags. Six had only one legible side, either the person's name or the bank, and the rest were illegible on both sides. With that accomplished, we turned our attention to other research.

"Who made the lockbox?" asked Leslie. "If we can figure out who manufactured the metal container and when, that would help us determine its potential age and that of the keys."

"Let's see." I turned the lockbox over and searched the outside. Then I looked inside. Since I couldn't find a logo or company name, I searched the internet for like images. "Here's one manufactured by Walker Turner Company, Inc., from the 1920s to the 1930s. The two images, inside and out, look just like ours—rectangular shape, size, and clasp design." I turned the computer to face Leslie so she could see the images.

"That's the one!" she said. "So now we know the keys could have been in the lockbox as early as 1920. If Derick found the box in 1948, that means it was there between eighteen to twenty-eight years before he found it."

"And if they're Capone's keys, somehow, they wound up on the island around 1930, and he didn't come back for them. Something must have happened."

"Yeah," said Leslie, eyeing me curiously. "That 'something' was syphilis."

"Syphilis! Eww. Isn't that an STD that eats your brain?" My face scrunched as though I'd swallowed sour milk.

"Look the word up, Tootsie. That's why you have a computer."

I clicked a few keys.

"The website says Al Capone contracted syphilis, a sexually transmitted disease, in 1918 when he was around nineteen, but doctors didn't diagnose him through a Wassermann test until he was incarcerated in Atlanta in 1931. At that time, the level was a two on a four-point scale. But by 1938, while he was in Alcatraz, Capone displayed signs of confusion, combative and compulsive behavior, and wandering consciousness. It says they gave him another syphilis test, and that time the level was over four!"

"Oh, my!" said Leslie, slapping her cheeks.

"The article goes on to say Capone spent the rest of his term in the prison hospital under treatment until given early discharge in 1939 because of his health. He died of a stroke in 1948 at his Palm Island estate in Miami Beach."

"And syphilis? What does Wiki say about that?"

"Hmm. Not a very nice ailment. The article says the disease can invade the nervous system at any stage of infection and, in the later stages, can cause dementia. Seems that's what Capone had—severe dementia."

"There wasn't any treatment?"

"Let me see." I continued to read the article. "Here it is. Mercury treated syphilis until the discovery of penicillin in 1928. But apparently, the antibiotic wasn't available in medicinal form until 1942. By that time, most antibiotics went to the military to treat wounded soldiers and amputees in World War Two. The article states penicillin wasn't widely available to the public until 1947."

"Much too late to do Capone any good. No wonder he couldn't find the lockbox after he got out of prison, if indeed the lockbox was his. By that time, his brain was mush."

"Okay, so we know about Capone and his syphilis, but what does that have to do with the keys? Who are all these people, and what's in the safe deposit boxes? And the most important question of all, what connection did these keys have to Mr. Eastway's death?" What had been an uneventful morning was now pregnant with intrigue.

"I'll make arrangements for us to visit the park and take a tour," said Leslie. "Maybe we'll get lucky and find some information there."

"And I'll look for a book on Capone. Between the two of us, we should be able to figure out if the lockbox belonged to him and why he buried the container on the island. We know the keys go to safe deposit boxes in banks, but we don't know where the banks are. I'll research the banks, and we'll probably need to speak with Mrs. Eastway again after that. I'm sure we'll have plenty of questions for her."

Leslie got on her phone, and I went online with my computer.

The Deerfield Beach Historical Society recommended three books on Capone. The first was a book on the history of Deerfield Beach that included the island, the second was on Capone's time in Florida, and the third was a biography of the Chicago kingpin. I ordered all three in hopes they would shed some light on our mystery.

"We can get to Deerfield Island Park by taking a launch across the Hillsboro Canal on Saturdays or Sundays from Sullivan Park, a little jetty of land by the Hillsborough Bridge. I've made reservations for us next Saturday at 2:00 p.m. I can't wait." Leslie was always up for a good caper.

As I gathered the baggies to place them back in the lockbox, half of them slid from my grasp onto the kitchen floor.

"Slippery little devils, aren't they," Leslie remarked, walking toward the door.

"Plastic bags always are," I said, picking up the scattered baggies and tossing them back into the lockbox. "Heading home?"

"I'm going to look through my stash of documents and see if I can come up with anything more on Capone Island. Those boxes I've accumulated must have an article in them somewhere." Leslie made her way out the back to her house.

"They haven't let us down so far," I called after her, remembering the valuable information they'd supplied in our past capers.

Leslie's house was a maze of cardboard boxes and plastic tubs stuffed to the gills with historic photos, documents, newspaper articles, and the like she'd collected from her decades of living in Boca Raton. Except for the kitchen, only a narrow walkway allowed her to get from one room to another. Some people called accumulating such items hoarding; she called it storing. I asked her why she didn't donate the items to the Boca Raton Historical Society. She claimed she couldn't put her hands on things when she needed them if she did. In her defense, our first two capers proved her right. Still, I couldn't help but think she was comforted by having all that history surrounding her.

~

"Well, at least this mystery hasn't turned up any dead bodies." Connor, wearing his work-around-the-house clothes—khaki shorts and a blue T-shirt, both speckled with paint—gazed at me with raised eyebrows.

"Except for Mr. Eastway, according to his wife, and I hope this caper stays body empty. I've had enough dead bodies this past year to last me a lifetime. Can you help with the key tags?" I picked up a baggie and waggled it.

"Sure. My buddy Curtis Canfield can probably figure this out, but I'd need to send him the physical keys. He has to have the real thing to use his special lighting and photography."

"I suppose that would be okay. We'll keep the ones we can read and pack up the others. He doesn't need to know anything about them, does he? Like where they came from or who they're associated with?" I closed the lid on the lockbox.

"Nah, but the process might take a while, and we'd need to pay him since he'll be doing this on his own time."

"Of course. What about the lockbox itself? Do you think there could be any DNA evidence on that after all these years?"

"The integrity of fingerprints on the lockbox has probably been compromised after it being buried for so long and handled by so many people. The keys, though, are another story. If you and Leslie didn't touch them and neither did Mrs. Eastway, then perhaps they'll have some evidence on them. Maybe a good fingerprint or two. I'm sure the government has Capone's fingerprint card in their archives from his imprisonment. If Curtis can pull a print off the keys or tags, he might be able to match them to the ones on file."

"Wouldn't that be something?" I wiggled my eyebrows.

"Just let me know when you're ready to send them off. In the meantime, I still have lots of work to do on the cottage if my parents are to have an extended stay. And you can't spend all your time on this. With all the programming, taping, and editing you're doing in the studio, you've got your hands full, too. Mrs. Romero, how did we get so busy?" Connor lifted my chin. A lock of hair fell over his dark eyes as they searched mine before he found my lips in one of his hot, passionate kisses.

"I don't know," I said, feeling heat creep up my neck. "But I hope we're never too busy to enjoy this." I returned the kiss. He took my hand to lead me up the stairs toward our honeymoon suite—my parents' former bedroom I renovated before our impromptu wedding.

Our feet never touched the first step. The couch in the living room provided an adequate substitute.

Chapter 3

The next few days flew by. Between overseeing the crafting program tapings at the studio and Archie's upholstery and ministry shows, I went online and looked at dozens of websites regarding the banking industry. I even found a website with the Florida banking industry's complete history, so I started there while waiting for the print books to arrive. I quickly recognized, though, I'd probably need to speak with someone in the banking industry as there were just too many questions without answers.

Saturday introduced a bright, sunny, March morning after an overnight cold front saturated our parched South Florida landscape with rain. Residents welcomed the storm as we hadn't seen a drop of rain for over three weeks. Unfortunately, the overnight storm also brought me a headache and slight nausea. I'd had headaches before, even migraines, but never coupled with nausea. I splashed water on my face, rationalizing my symptoms were nothing more than a result of the change in weather and would go away. After several hours, they did.

Leslie and I toggled our windows down as we drove south on US1, then east on Hillsboro Boulevard to Sullivan Park in Deerfield Beach. The air smelled fresh and sweet as it blew through our hair and the car. Turning into the park, I pulled to a stop in front of a meter where a sign said we had four free hours, ample time to stroll through the park, catch the launch on the north side, and tour the island.

As we meandered through the grounds on the winding path and past the splash park, we came upon a bronze plaque on a coquina pedestal that gave the park's history. Initially, the land that jutted into the Intracoastal Waterway was a Tequesta Indian campground between Lake Okeechobee and the Atlantic, where the Indians overnighted while hunting and fishing. According to the plaque, these indigenous people occupied Southeast Florida five thousand years ago and preceded the Seminole Indians by centuries.

The ride across the Hillsboro Canal from Sullivan Park to the island took less than ten minutes. The air smelled clean and salty as a cool breeze swept over us even though the sun brought warmth to my cheeks as I tilted my face toward the golden orb. When we docked at the park marina, David Caldwell, who appeared in his late seventies, greeted us in a Friends of Deerfield Island Park green T-shirt and name tag. He would serve as our Ambassador for the afternoon.

While others who came over in the launch took off down a boardwalk and headed into the mangrove swamp to the west, Leslie and I were David's only tour guests. His tall frame, beset with a friendly face and blue eyes that crinkled at the edges when he smiled, towered over both of us as he smiled warmly. I could see the man had been quite the looker in his day. He still was.

"So, what brings you ladies to the park this afternoon?" David's voice was friendly and sincere.

Leslie and I looked at each other and shared a smile.

"Just out for a ramble on such a beautiful day," I said, hoping to keep our real intention close to the vest.

"And trying to solve a mystery," said Leslie. Her gaze at David lingered, as did her upturned lips.

"A mystery, huh?" David leaned in toward Leslie. "Maybe I can help. Retired Air Force Colonel—intelligence," he said in a soft voice just above a whisper.

My stare danced between Leslie and David, whose eyes locked onto each other like the proverbial 'love at first sight' cliché. I watched as a bloom of pink spread across Leslie's cheeks.

Is something going on here? They just met!

"Uh, I think we'd better stick to the tour, David," I said, wrapping an arm around Leslie's shoulders and ushering her reluctantly down the path.

"Of course," he said, shaking his daze and catching up with us. "Let's start with the history of the island."

David gave us a brief overview of the island from its early days as vacant land and the Indians that occupied the area to the dredging of the Hillsboro Canal and Intracoastal in the early 1900s. Spoilage from the dredging expanded the size of the peninsula.

"Right where you took the launch on Sullivan Island, there used to be a small packing house. That's where Al Capone operated a little 'fish business' during Prohibition in the mid-1920s. At the time, he was the boss of the Chicago Outfit and brought illegal booze in from the Bahamas and Cuba up the inlet from the Hillsboro Lighthouse to the packing house. He'd fill the bottom of barrels with liquor, cover the bottles with a false top, pack the rest of the container with dry ice and fish from local fishermen, and ship the barrels north to Chicago on the Florida East Coast Railroad. The authorities were none the wiser," said David, a smug look to his face.

"How exciting." Leslie silently clapped and looked at me as though everything the man said was the most fascinating thing she'd ever heard.

I rolled my eyes.

She's a historian, for heaven's sake! She's probably heard that story a dozen times.

"So, he owned the island as early as 1925?" I asked.

"No, no," corrected David, "Capone leased the packing house and didn't purchase this property until 1930 when he bought the parcel in the name of his Miami attorney Vincent Giblin. Of course, the land was still a peninsula then and didn't become an island until the mid-1950s."

"If Capone put the property in the name of his attorney, how do people know the land really belonged to the gangster?" asked Leslie, her historian demand for proof kicking in.

"Official documents in the Broward County Courthouse regarding the land purchase show Giblin signed the document, but everyone understood Capone was the money behind the purchase. He registered all his houses, vehicles, businesses, and personal property in other people's names—his wife, brother, attorney, and so forth. History shows us that Capone owned very few items in his name for fear of being apprehended by the government. For his personal purchases, he carried cash and loads of the green stuff," said David.

"So, are you saying that even bank accounts weren't in his name?" I wanted to make sure I heard him correctly.

"That's right. Everything Capone owned was registered in someone else's name. Of course, he counted on the premise that no one would dare double-cross him. He was right," said David.

I looked at Leslie with raised eyebrows. If Capone didn't want the Treasury Department to trace the property or money back to him, the fact that the key tags to the safe deposit boxes had other people's names on them made loads of sense. Yet, I was now more fascinated than ever to discover who these people were, their relationship to Capone, and what was in the safe deposit boxes. Did they all contain the same thing?

"Why'd he want the land way up here? He had a lovely home in Miami Beach," said Leslie.

"Ah, yes, but like the reason he left Chicago, Capone was tired of being harassed by authorities and planned to build a large home here. The location was the perfect spot—fifty-five acres of isolated land surrounded by water. What could be more private?"

"So, what happened to the land after Capone went to jail?" I asked.

"When he couldn't pay the taxes, the land reverted back to the original owner. When the owner defaulted on his taxes, the bank took over the parcel. Later, the land became the property of Broward County. Now, how'd you two like to see the mangrove swamp along the boardwalk? Lots of wildlife." David directed us toward the elevated wooden boardwalk that wound through the mangroves and a forest of cypress trees along the west and north sides of the island.

After a pleasant walk and David's explanation of the island's flora and fauna, the boardwalk emerged onto a sandy path that looped through the rest of the island and came out to a small, sandy beach. As we returned to our starting point, we passed a butterfly garden of red pentas and pink milkweed, along with a giant bronze tortoise named Tony, the mascot and icon of the island, a designated sanctuary for land tortoises. After a couple of hours, our tour ended, and we bid goodbye to David and Deerfield Island Park, a.k.a. Capone Island.

"Well, Tootsie, seems we might be on the right track considering what David told us about Capone never owning anything in his own name. Might be the reason there are so many different names on the tags," said Leslie as we drove back to Boca.

"I'm hoping the books I ordered give me some more information regarding this, and who knows? Maybe there are some names in those books that correspond to the key tags."

Just then, Leslie's cell phone rang. She looked at the caller ID, then me, and twisted her back slightly as though she didn't want me to see the display. She spoke in a low, muffled voice, unusual for her.

"Me, too. Sure, tomorrow would be fine. I'll talk to you later," she said, quickly ending the call.

"Don't tell me that was David." I looked at Leslie and grinned. "How in the world did he get your phone number?"

"Remember when you went to the restroom?" she asked in a shy voice. "He asked me for my number then."

"I see. Well, he's a handsome man, you're both single, and over twenty-one. See where the attraction goes." Being a widow must have been challenging for Leslie after fifty-seven years of marriage.

"I don't know, Tootsie. He's a younger man, and I haven't had a date since Howard died ten years ago."

"Age shouldn't matter, not when you're in your golden years. And he's not asking you to marry him. He only wants to get to know you better. Besides, what are you always telling me?"

"Life is for the living!" we said in unison, sharing a hearty laugh.

"Oh, my!" said Leslie, cupping her cheeks in her trembling hands. "What if things go well and he wants to see me again? If things get serious, he'll want to come over. What am I going to do about the house?"

"Maybe David wanting to see you is a good thing. The possibility of his coming over will give you the incentive to rethink the boxes in the hallways and rooms."

"I'll have to meet him somewhere else until I can figure something out." Panic infused her voice.

"Calm down, Leslie. When you get to the place where you want to have David over, Connor and I will help you reorganize everything."

I left Leslie off at her house, but I could tell she was still conflicted about seeing David—excited yet apprehensive.

~

Around mid-week, I packed up the keys and sent them off to Connor's forensic lab technician buddy for deciphering. I then turned my attention to reading the books that arrived. I needed to figure out if the keys really did belong to Al Capone, though I didn't know if the books held the answer. Still, I needed to find out as much as possible.

In preparation for reading Capone's biography, I studied the names on my list of key tags several times to familiarize myself with them in case I ran across one of the names in the book. We could easily make out three women and two men's names on the five key tags we could read. What we needed to do was match the bank's location to the proximity of the person.

My favorite place to read was tucked into bed with Bigfoot purring beside me. So that night, I slipped under the covers and opened the first book. It gave me a good history of Capone Island and documented in endnotes what David said about the island having been purchased by Capone in attorney Giblin's name. Original documents still resided in the Broward County Courthouse to authenticate that fact, as David said.

Since Capone's first trip to Florida was in 1925, the same year he took over the Chicago Outfit from Frank Torrio, I figured some of the keys could have been put in the box that early. These were most likely from Chicago banks. Since he moved to Miami permanently in 1927, purchasing the house on Palm Island in Miami Beach in 1928, that gave him ample time, from 1927 to when he was arrested in 1930, to open safe deposit boxes anywhere from Miami to Deerfield Beach. Not to mention he returned to Chicago upon occasion and could have more deposit boxes up there. And what if he opened a safety deposit box in Miami in the name of a person who lived in Chicago or New York? That would throw a monkey wrench into the whole quest. Much research still needed to be done, including finding a genealogist who could research the names to see if relatives existed. This investigation would be a daunting task, but I knew just who to contact to lead us to the right genealogist.

"Hey, Randi," said Rachel, answering my call. She'd been my best friend since high school, was acquainted with everyone in the city, and served as COO of my production studio. "Where have you been? That new husband of yours keeping you undercover?" She snickered at her double entendre.

"Well, if you stayed in the office long enough, you'd probably see me," I said. "On second thought, don't stay in the office. If you did, we wouldn't have so many sponsors, and the productions wouldn't be going so smoothly. So, please, stay away. But, seriously, I do miss our time together. When can we have a girls' night out?"

"Soon, I promise. Now, I know you didn't call me just to make a dinner date. What's on your mind?"

I could never fool Rachel. She understood me better than anyone.

"I'm looking for a genealogist. Know anyone good?"

"Uh oh. Sounds like another caper. What's up this time?" Rachel's voice sounded apprehensive.

"Capone's keys."

"Huh?"

"Never mind. I'll tell you all about them when we go out. Dangling the explanation like a lure will give you some incentive to get together with me. In the meantime, I need an excellent genealogist. Someone who can think outside the box."

"Well, as usual, you've come to the right place. I just finished having a family tree completed, and I highly recommend her. Mandy O'Brien is her name. She's as Irish as they come, has a wicked sense of humor, and really knows her stuff. I'll text you her number."

A few seconds later, I received Rachel's text.

"You're the best," I told her.

"Don't forget to remind the kids of that the next time you see them. They think I'm a helicopter mom."

"Can't afford not to be in this world. Thanks for the info. Let me know when you can pull yourself away from the kids and that handsome husband of yours. Dinner will be on me."

"Sushi?"

"You got it," I confirmed.

~

When I got to the studio the following morning, I wanted to call Mandy, but fatigue overwhelmed me. I could hardly pick up the phone as I sat at my desk. What was going on? First nausea and headaches, now fatigue? I went to the restroom and looked at myself in the mirror. My eyes did look a bit glassy. Was I getting a cold? The flu?

I slogged through taping and editing all afternoon, though I could hardly concentrate. When I returned home, I found Bigfoot munching on his kibbles in the kitchen while Connor prepared dinner—grilled salmon with brown rice, asparagus, and a mixed fruit cup. I gave him a generous kiss.

"Do I have time to swim laps for a half-hour before dinner?" Swimming had been my passion in high school. Not only was I on the swim team, but I also worked on weekends as a lifeguard. Since returning to Boca Grande, I continued to swim laps as often as possible to keep in shape, plus they always seemed to reenergize me.

"Sure, though you'll have to ask Bigfoot if he minds. He's been restless all day waiting for you to come home."

"And what about you, Mr. Romero? Have you been restless all day, waiting for me, too?"

"What do you think?" Connor pulled me to him and ran kisses up my neck.

After dinner, Bigfoot and I wandered over to Leslie's. I hadn't spoken to her for a few days and wanted to know how her "date" went with David.

"So, what happened on your date?" I sat on the edge of my chair at her dinette in great anticipation of her response.

"We had a nice evening."

I pulled back and stared at her. "That's all? You had a nice evening?"

"Truth be told, the date was more than nice," she said.

"Come on, spill the beans." I sat forward, eyes wide. "I want every detail."

"We went to Max's Grille in Mizner Park for dinner. Then we walked around and window shopped."

"And?" I gestured with my hands for her to continue.

"Then I came home."

"What? No goodnight kiss? No plans to see him again?" I was baffled.

"I didn't say that. Our time together was pleasant, and I enjoyed the company of a charming man who loves history as much as I do."

"So, you'll be seeing him again."

"We have plans for the weekend, and he wants you and Connor to join us. He thinks we'd have a grand time together since both of the men have military backgrounds and were involved with information gathering."

"And just where are we going?"

"The south side of Lake Okeechobee. We're going to visit Belle Glade, Clewiston, and La Belle. There's some great history there. He wants to know more about Florida, and I haven't been back for decades," said Leslie.

"Neither have I, though Connor and I drove by Lake O when we went to Lake Placid while tracking down Raul Gonzales. But we didn't stop and see the lake. Hey, that just triggered something. I remember reading a newspaper article that Capone was interested in purchasing some land in that area to build a hunting and fishing lodge. Maybe we can find someone up there who may know about the potential purchase. The land may not have anything to do with the keys, but one never knows."

"I'll make a few phone calls and see if we can't set up appointments to speak with the local historians. I know most of them. But let's consider staying overnight, so we don't have to rush. Some great old homes are now B&Bs around there, and I think the trip may be too long for David and me for just one day."

"Good idea. I'll get with Connor and make plans. We'll drive, of course. All you'll have to do is sit in the back and get to know David better." I walked to the back door and was about to leave when I wheeled around. "Wait a minute! You didn't tell me. Did he kiss you?"

Leslie looked at me. A mischievous grin migrated across her lips.

"I see," I said, closing the door. A smile drifted across my lips as well.

When I got home, I called Mandy, the genealogist. Her voice was warm, and her Irish brogue accent delightful. I explained what I needed, and she said to email her the names and any further information I could supply. At this point, that was practically nil.

I figured we needed to tackle this mystery from several aspects—discover who the people were on the key tags, if the person lived in the same location as the bank, and what was inside the boxes. Since the boxes were issued so long ago, rentals most likely remained unpaid for years. After that, the banks probably confiscated the items or transferred them to a state repository for unclaimed property. An online search revealed that was precisely what happened in Florida:

"If the owner of the safety deposit box fails to pay the rental fee, the financial institution will drill the box and remove its contents. If the bank cannot locate the owner, after approximately three years, the contents are sent to the Florida Department of Financial Services, Division of Unclaimed Property."

To date, Florida still retained over one billion dollars in unclaimed property. The good news, though, was that there was no statute of limitations, and citizens had the right to claim their property at any time at no cost. That meant whatever was in the boxes still existed, and finding the relatives would prove vital to solving the mystery.

After finishing Capone's biography, I had three names that matched the key tags: Ilsa Carpuchi, a Brooklyn New York school teacher; Lena Galluccio, resident of New York; and Eleanor Patterson, owner of the *Times-Herald,* a Washington newspaper.

I couldn't say why these names, all women, stuck out, but at least we had something to start with. I forwarded these names to Mandy. I figured the process would take her days to get back to me. In the meantime, I'd finish up my week at the studio, and Connor and I, along with Leslie and David, would head to Lake O.

Chapter 4

We left early Saturday morning for the state's interior, but somehow the fatigue was still dogging me. As I rested my head against the head restraint. I was amazed at how sparse the terrain became once we left West Palm Beach's wealthy developments and moved into the rural landscape west of the city. As we drove toward Belle Glade on the south side of Florida's largest lake, the open skies and miles of land stretched before us as we whizzed by sugar cane and agricultural fields set in rich soil. That's why the town was endearingly referred to as Muck City.

Leslie gave us a brief history of the area and recounted the heartbreaking story of the Category 4 hurricane of 1928. Its winds, up to 150 miles per hour, pushed water against the south end of the levy surrounding Lake O, causing a breach. Twenty-foot-deep water flooded the agricultural community in places, killing more than 2,500 people south of the lake.

"All we'd need is one Category 3 or more hurricane to make a direct hit on South Florida, and we'd have double or triple those casualties. So far, South Florida has been pretty fortunate to miss the big ones, though Hurricane Andrew in 1992 did a lot of damage," continued Leslie.

"I was just a toddler, but I remember hiding in my parents' closest," I said. "The yard was a mess afterward, with downed branches and shredded foliage everywhere. Even Boca, away from the hurricane's center, had wind speeds around ninety miles an hour. Thankfully, early warning from the National Hurricane Center allowed most residents to evacuate the Miami area, but the physical damage ran well into the billions."

Belle Glade was a small town consisting mainly of migrant workers and welfare recipients. The men brought up in the area who successfully made their way out of poverty typically did so on the high school gridiron, obtaining football scholarships to colleges and then some moving on to the NFL.

We met Belle Glade historian Richard Salter at the library. A tall, thin man of color in his late sixties, Richard wore a white shirt and khaki pants with red suspenders.

"Y'all come this way to the conference room. I've got something to show you," he said in his Florida draw. He tettered from side to side as he walked, and we followed him down a short hall away from the main library filled with students at computers to a room with a conference table and ten chairs. "Y'all have a seat."

We did as instructed.

"Richard has lived in Belle Glade his entire life and worked in the sugar cane industry for thirty-five years before retiring," said Leslie. "Now he goes into the schools and shares Florida and the area's history with the students."

"It's important to make sure children appreciate where they come from. Of course, there's nothing more important than making sure they get a good education so that they can break the cycle of poverty. I try to help with that," said Richard.

"I'm sure the students appreciate your dedication to both the history and to them," I said.

"Sometimes." Richard emphasized the word with a high-pitched giggle. "But most of the time, they're more interested in playing video games and messin' around with social media or each other. Hard to keep their attention on the important things. I hope I'll reach some of them, and they'll find history interesting enough to want to pursue the topic on their own. But you didn't come to talk about education. I believe you wanted to know about Al Capone and his possible purchase of land in the area."

"We're hoping you might know about the transaction." Leslie sat forward, eager to hear what our host had to say.

"And you gentlemen? What's your role in all of this?" Richard's gaze bounced between Connor and David.

"I'm the chauffeur, and David is Leslie's sidekick," said Connor, jerking his thumb at David and smiling.

Richard laughed. "So, the ladies are heading up this one, huh?"

"Truer words don't exist," said David with a grin.

"Well, here we are. I found an article in the *Everglades News*, a newspaper published in Canal Point, a little town north of here. The article is the only document I've found on Al Capone's potential land purchase." Richard passed each of us a copy of the article.

Everglades News, Canal Point, (June 6, 1930)–Just days before Al Capone's padlocking trial in Miami, reports surfaced that the notorious gangster sent his attorney Vincent Giblin on a scouting trip to the east bank of Lake Okeechobee to look for property. W.G. "Guy" Stovall, publisher for a time of the "East Beach" newspaper, confirmed the report saying that he had traveled to Miami to present an offer to the beer baron to sell a block of land fronting on Lake Okeechobee. His understanding was that Capone and his friends wanted to purchase the land for a hunting and fishing preserve.

As I read the name "Guy Stovall," my eyes widened, and a tingle raced up my spine.

"Do you know if Capone ever followed through on the purchase?" I asked.

"Not that I know of. My understanding is he was also interested in land in the Deerfield Beach area," said Richard.

"He did purchase land there," said David, "but when he went to prison, he defaulted on the loan, and the county eventually took the property back. The fifty-five-acre site is now called Deerfield Island Park, run by Broward County."

"Ahh," said Richard, nodding.

"Do you know the exact location of the property Capone wanted?" I asked.

Richard tapped the clipping with his index finger. "From the paper's description, the property sounds as though it was located just north of Canal Point."

"Does the *Everglades News* still exist?" asked Leslie.

"No, ma'am. The paper went out of publication in 1967." Richard looked at each of us, expecting another question.

"What do you know about this man Stovall? Any relatives in the area?" I hoped he'd say 'yes.'

"People who have been in this area for any time have lots of relatives around these parts. I don't know any of the Stovalls personally, but some still live in the Canal Point area. I'm sure you can find them through the internet or check with the Chamber of Commerce. I believe Stovall sold real estate on the side. That's how he got involved with the property. But I need to warn you, I understand the family is very private and not so friendly. I don't know if any of them would even talk to you."

"Well, thanks for the heads up," I said. "You've been more than helpful, and we appreciate your time."

We all rose and shook Richard's hand in goodbye. I hooked my arm in Leslie's and walked her out; the men followed.

"Stovall is one of the names on the key tags," I said, hardly able to contain my excitement once we got into the car. "The name isn't one of those in Capone's biography, but it is on one of the tags."

"How fabulous! At least we can give Mandy another name and see if any of Stovall's relatives show up as a result," Leslie said.

"What tags?" asked David.

"Ladies, I think you've gotten yourselves into a real legal mess here," said Connor. He started the car and pulled out of the parking lot, heading for Clewiston.

"What do you mean?" I was well aware this wouldn't be easy, but a legal mess?

"Think about this for a minute. First, there's the question of who owns the lockbox. Was the box really Capone's? If the answer is 'yes' and the contents obtained through ill-gotten gains, such as his brothels, speakeasies, or other illicit sources, whatever is in the safety deposit boxes belongs to Uncle Sam. Then you've got Derek Eastway, who found the box. Would his relatives have a legal claim to the lockbox and contents, even though his wife honored his wishes and gave the box to you? And what about the keys with different names on the tags? If Capone isn't established as the rightful owner, then the people whose names are on the key tags would be the next in line. And since they are deceased, their heirs could lay claim to the contents of that particular safety deposit box."

"What tags?" David asked with emphasis for a second time and a little bit louder.

Suddenly, I realized we'd been talking freely in front of him, someone we didn't yet know very well. Plus, how rude of us to talk about the topic and exclude him from the conversation.

"So sorry, David. We're working on that mystery Leslie mentioned at the park," I said in an off-handed way.

"You mean Capone's buried lockbox?"

We all fell silent.

"You know about that?" asked Leslie.

"Sure. Haven't you read the book by Capone's niece? She's the one who mentions the lockbox. According to her, Uncle Al stashed one hundred million dollars in cash for his retirement in different safety deposit boxes, then gathered the keys into one lockbox and buried the container just before he went to prison. When he got out, he couldn't remember where he'd buried the darn thing. Even his brother, Ralph, got involved and had the Outfit dig up his brother's estates in Chicago and Palm Island. When they came up empty, he had Al hypnotized. They never did find the lockbox. Are you saying you have it?"

I swallowed and squirmed a bit in my seat. "Leslie and I like to find interesting mysteries and try to solve them. Most of our work is simply hypothetical."

"Then how could Stovall's name get on one of the key tags?" asked David.

"We don't know," said Leslie in resignation. "That's what we're trying to find out."

For a while, we drove without conversation as we headed toward Clewiston, paralleling the thirty-foot-high Hoover Dike that surrounded the lake. Since we couldn't see the water from the road, we turned off US 27 after the Miami Canal and drove up a ramp into John Stretch Memorial Park. There we found a lovely area with complete amenities—picnic tables, boat ramp, a small lake for canoeing and kayaking, access to the Lake Okeechobee scenic trail that winds around the entire lake, and more. Due to a large marshy area, though, we couldn't see the vast lake.

"I know this is none of my business, but if you let me in on your little mystery, I may be able to help. I know a lot of people in government who I can call upon if needed," said David after we stretched our legs.

"Let's continue to Clewiston," said Connor. "We can have lunch there and talk further."

In Clewiston, we all piled out of the car and slipped under the large sign that depicted a red, green, and blue macaw parrot and the words *Scotty's Tiki Bar*. One side of the large outdoor covered patio, with its wooden floor, exposed beam ceiling, and open sides, was taken up by a rectangular wooden bar. Tables and chairs for dining took up the rest of the space. A narrow strip of concrete on the southeast side of the patio next to a canal offered outside seating. Since the weather was a clear day with warm sun, we opted to sit at an outdoor table with an umbrella to take in the view of the canal and the jumping carp.

"Tell us a little about yourself," said Connor to David after we ordered drinks.

"I suppose that's in order since I asked in on your mystery. I served in Air Force intelligence for twenty-five years. I worked at the Pentagon and developed professional and personal relationships with several congressmen and women, many of whom are still in the House and Senate. I can't reveal the intimate nature of my duties, but I had top-secret clearance and dealt with highly classified information."

"So you know how to keep a secret," said Connor, grinning.

"To the death." David crossed his heart and held his open palm in a swear position. "But I don't expect you to take my word. I understand you're in the investigative field, a former CID Special Agent. You'll probably want to check me out."

"I don't think our capers deal with anything that sensitive, at least not to the general public, but we do try to keep our escapades just between us," said Leslie.

"What brought you to Florida?" I asked.

"The weather. Isn't that why everyone comes here? After my wife's death a couple of years ago, I needed something to do to keep busy. While not as torturous as in the New England states, the winters in Washington can be challenging at times. I wanted a place where I could be outdoors all year around. I'd had enough of months on end of gray winter skies."

"I certainly understand about those prolonged gray skies in Washington. So much nicer to look out your window and see sunshine." I didn't miss Washington at all.

"Once I got here, I looked for something to keep me occupied and found Friends of Deerfield Island Park. Heck, the place is right across the canal from my condo. I looked at the property every day but didn't know a volunteer group assisted in the care of the park. On the island, nature surrounds me, and I enjoy educating visitors about the park. I do miss the intrigue of my former job with the Air Force, but the job brought a lot of stress as well," said David.

"Our condolences on the loss of your wife," said Connor. "Seems like a lot of losses around this table. Leslie lost her husband about ten years ago, and Randi lost both her parents a year ago when a drug dealer mistakenly pushed their car into a canal."

"Now everything makes sense," said David, slapping the palm of his hand to his forehead. "You're the Randi Brooks who owns that fabric store and the one who found the statues. I saw you on TV and read the stories online. You'd think someone in the intelligence field would have figured that out sooner."

"I try to keep a low profile," I said.

The server returned with our drinks, and we all ordered lunch. The rest of the conversation dealt with us trying to get to know David better and him trying to know us better. By the time we got back in the car, everyone seemed very comfortable with David.

"If I may make a suggestion," said David as we drove toward the Clewiston Museum. "Instead of going to La Belle, I think we should head back toward Belle Glade tomorrow and try to find Mr. Stovall's relatives in Pahokee. We probably need time tonight to do a little research to see if he still has family in the area and cement our approach. Plus, we could all use a good night's sleep. What do you think?"

"Sounds like a plan. I'll phone the closest visitor center or Chamber of Commerce later and see what I can find out." I fingered through my phone and wrote myself a note of reminder.

We pulled into the parking lot of the Clewiston Museum and toured the pictorial history of the sugar cane industry as well as a remarkable array of prehistoric fossils of animals that lived in Florida thirty million years ago—saber tooth tiger, wooly mammoth, mastodon, giant armadillo. Then we checked into the Clewiston Inn, built in 1938, and had a pleasant dinner before tucking into bed. Over breakfast, we discussed our drive back toward Belle Glade and up the east side of Lake O to Pahokee and Canal Point.

"Canal Point only has about five hundred residents, so I doubt they have a Chamber or Visitor's Center. They do have a post office, though, so we might get some information there," I said, looking at my phone.

"Postal employees aren't allowed to give out information about their customers, so getting anything out of them might be difficult," said Connor.

"What about Pahokee?" asked David.

"The city has a much larger population and has a Chamber of Commerce," said Connor, having accessed the city information on his phone. "My suggestion is that we let David and Leslie take the lead on asking the questions. Otherwise, they might think Randi and I are reporters or the media, looking for a story. You need to find out whether the Stovall family still lives in the area and if they have any contact info. If all else fails, you may need to say something about an inheritance, and you must find the relatives. Kind of like what the authorities do to track down those who have jumped bail or criminals in hiding. The lure of money works every time." He looked at us with raised brows.

"Sounds good to me," said David. "What do you think, Leslie? Can you play the wife of an old man looking to give some money away?"

"You have no idea what a good actress I can be," she said. "We'll just be the old couple trying to make sure the inheritance gets to the right people."

"Great. Then we're all set. Randi and I will wait for you in the car." Connor looked at me and nodded.

We packed into the car and drove to Pahokee. The Chamber resided in a one-story ochre-colored block building that looked of the 1950s vintage. Connor parked around the block while David and Leslie, using her cane for added effect, walked to the entrance. About ten minutes later, they returned and got into the car. Their beaming smiles spoke of success.

"Piece of cake, and Leslie was right. She is a good actor." David put his arm around her shoulders and kissed her on the cheek. "Just to stay in character," he said. Leslie blushed.

"So…what's the scoop?" I asked.

"Fortunately, we hit upon an old-timer with the Chamber. He said some of the Stovall family still lives here. He gave us the name of Thelma Stovall, Guy's great-niece," said David.

"She's elderly, never married, and lives alone. We got her phone number." Leslie waved a piece of paper at us.

"Let's give the ole' gal a call and see if she's up for visitors," said Connor.

We didn't know what to expect—a lovely older woman or someone involved with Derick Eastway's death.

Chapter 5

L eslie put in the call to Thelma. Fortunately, she was home.
"Ms. Stovall? This is Leslie Davidson. I'm a historian from Boca Raton and am in town today doing some research. If it wouldn't be imposing, I'd love to stop by or meet you somewhere to speak to you about your great uncle Guy Stovall...So glad you're available...I do have three others with me, but if having all of us in your home would be inconvenient, I'll just come by myself...You're sure you don't mind?...Great...And your address...205 Park Street...We'll be there shortly, Ms. Stovall. Thank you."

"We need to know more about Guy and why Capone included his name on one of the keys. Hopefully, Thelma can shed some light on this." I always tried to keep an optimistic outlook.

Connor punched Thelma's address into our GPS, and we took off. Pahokee wasn't that large a town, so we didn't find navigating to Thelma's very difficult. We pulled into the driveway in front of a small, well-kept home with white vinyl siding. She was a gardener by the looks of the care Thelma took of her yard. Her small, but colorful gardens of roses, pentas, and variegated ground cover surrounded by low white picket fences spoke of loving care.

"Leslie, you and David go first and introduce yourselves to Thelma. We don't want to all go up there and overwhelm her. If she feels comfortable with us coming too, just give us a wave," said Connor.

"Okey-dokey," replied Leslie.

She and David looked at each other, took a deep breath, and walked up to the front door. Connor and I watched as a white-haired woman wearing beige pants and a floral print shirt appeared behind a screen door. After a short conversation, Leslie waved to us.

Following introductions, Thelma, who seemed in her mid-nineties yet still quite spry, led us through a small foyer and into a comfortable living room.

"I ain't had this many guests in years. Sit down." She gestured to an antique love seat and side chairs. Though she spoke with a Florida drawl and slurred some of her words because of her lack of teeth, we could easily understand her.

"Thank you," said Leslie. She sat on the loveseat; David sat beside her.

"How about some sweet iced tea? Just made some with fresh mint from my garden." Thelma gave us a toothless grin and gazed at each of us, looking for takers.

"Well, I, for one, would love tea with fresh mint. Haven't had any in ages." Leslie smiled and nodded.

"How about y'all?" asked Thelma, pointing to the rest of us. Our hands went up.

"Ms. Stovall, let me help you." Connor rose and followed Thelma's petite frame into the kitchen.

I could hear the clink of glasses and ice, the pouring of tea, and muffled conversation as I perused Thelma's clean and orderly home. A fireplace stood in the center of one wall, the mantle covered in photos of what I figured were relatives. Perhaps one was a photo of great uncle Guy. Above the fireplace was a large horizontal oil painting of a path leading to a lake. A stately Royal Poinciana tree with its unmistakable lacy canopy and red-orange blooms arched gracefully over the pathway on one side of the lane.

"I'll bet that's an original Florida Highwaymen painting," said Leslie with unbridled curiosity. She rose and inspected the painting close up. "Yep. The scene is painted on masonite, framed with crown molding, and there's the signature—Harold Newton. He was one of the original Highwaymen. This painting is easily worth five to ten thousand dollars."

David let out a whistle. "Who were the Highwaymen?"

"Only the most prolific group of self-taught Black landscape artists in Florida, maybe even the country," said Leslie, standing back and admiring the piece. "They sold their work along the coast of Florida, mostly in the Fort Pierce area. They walked up and down A1A and Federal Highway from about 1950 to the late 1970s. That's how they got their name. Of course, their offspring still exist, and many paint, but most of the original twenty-six Highwaymen are deceased. Their beautiful paintings live on, like this one, and are now collector items."

Indeed, the image was vibrant and eye-catching. I'd seen other paintings by the Highwaymen that included scenes of the Everglades, beaches, palm trees, sunsets, and the like. Each was just as striking as the next.

"Here we are," said Connor, carrying a tray of glasses filled with tea.

49

Everyone took their seats. Thelma placed a glass of tea on a coaster along with a napkin in front of each of us. Then she sat in an overstuffed contemporary recliner that seemed out of place and too big for the room. The chair was angled so she could see the TV.

"Mmm. Wonderful tea," said Leslie.

"Cain't have tea without mint," said Thelma with a slight chuckle. "So, ya'll come to ask me about Uncle Guy?"

"Yes," said Leslie in her soft, inquisitive style. "I understand he owned a newspaper and sold real estate on the side."

Thelma brought a hand to her mouth and let out a hearty laugh. "Did more than that, honey. Them were Prohibition days. Why if it weren't for Guy, everyone 'round here would've died of thirst. He brought the good stuff in all the way from the Bahamas and hid it in the lake attached to buoys until needed. If they didn't want the good stuff, he'd sell 'em moonshine he produced out yonder in the backwoods. Yesiree, Guy was what you'd call 'a jack of all trades.' Had to be back then to make a livin'." She sat back and took a long drink of her tea.

"Ms. Thelma, I understand that your great uncle had an opportunity to sell some land to Al Capone sometime around 1930. The article I read said he wanted to use the land for a fishing and hunting retreat. Do you know anything about that?" I asked.

Thelma sat upright. "Do I know anything about that? Sure thing. I was only three, but I'll never forget the day ole' Scarface came to Pahokee. No, wait. First, his attorney came here lookin' for land. I think his name was Giblet."

"Giblin," corrected David.

"Oh, that's right." Thelma slapped her knee and chuckled. "I wanted to remember his name, so I always thought of chicken giblet gravy. After Giblin saw what he wanted, ole' Scarface himself came up."

~

June 1930

A shiny black car with three male passengers pulled to the curb in front of Guy Stovall's modest newspaper office—a small, one-room storefront tucked between Edna's Diner and Pop's sundry. The driver—a large man in height and width with a square face carved by hard lines—opened the back door. A second man stepped out about the same size as the driver but with a chubby face. He wore dark pants and a short-sleeved, light-blue shirt open at the collar. His armpits sported dark circles, and his torso splotches of sweat. Following him, a third man who was taller and thinner stepped out. Due to the incessant heat, both men left their ties and jackets in the car.

"Stay here. This will only take a minute," said the second man to the driver.

"Sure, Boss," the driver responded in a baritone voice.

The second man walked toward the building, casually chatting with the third man. Both men lifted their heads and sniffed the air, detecting the odor of grease from the chicken frying at Edna's. As they opened the door and stepped into the small office, two open windows and the whir of a fan mixed the smell of ink with that of the grease. The combination made for an unpleasant odor. The entrance, separated by a waist-high railing, formed a lobby. Behind the barrier, a printing press cranked out pieces of paper. Two men took the pages and placed them into stacks. A towheaded toddler sat on the floor in the corner, playing with her Raggedy Ann doll.

"You Guy Stovall?" called the second man over the groan of the press.

"That's me," yelled Guy, looking up. He rubbed his hands clean on a cloth and stepped up to the railing.

"I'm Al Brown from Miami, and this is my attorney, Vincent Giblin. We're here to see the property in Canal Point." Brown, stuck out his hand.

"Sure enough." Guy shook hands with both men. *"Hey Leo, turn off the press,"* Guy called over his shoulder. Leo complied. When Guy turned around, he saw for the first time that the man in front of him had two scars on his left cheek and another just under his shirt collar. *"Brown"* wasn't the man's real name. Guy had read the papers, seen the photos—Al Capone, a.k.a. Scarface. A shiver ran through him.

"You can go with us. My driver is outside," said Brown.

"Up to you. I just need to take my niece with me. Babysitting, you know." Guy went to his desk, pulled a .38 from the top drawer, and stuck the gun into the back of his pants. *"Protection,"* he said when he saw Brown and Giblin staring at him.

"Against what?" asked Giblin.

"Rattlesnakes, alligators, cougar, bear, hogs, you name it," said Guy before scooping up Thelma.

Guy sat in the front seat with Thelma and her doll on his lap to point the driver toward the property. Brown and Giblin sat in the back. After several miles on a gravel road, the car turned off onto a roadbed of packed sand surrounded by tall palmetto and scrub brush. After another couple of miles, they stopped in a clearing just big enough for a tight turnaround.

"Well, this is ninety-five acres of good hunting land with access to the lake for fishing," said Guy. He got out of the car with Thelma in his arms.

Brown and Giblin got out, too. The two men followed Guy and Thelma down a sandy path and up a rise. When they reached the top, Brown realized they were standing on the dike around Lake Okeechobee. He stood next to Guy, hands on his hips, and did a three-sixty, inspecting the land behind him—thick scrub, pines, palmetto, and underbrush—and Lake Okeechobee in front. The lake was so vast, even though he squinted, Brown couldn't see the other side.

"It looks like an ocean," said Brown. "Good fishing?"

"The best," Guy said. "Largemouth bass, bluegill, redear sunfish, and crappie. For hunting, you got deer, hogs, and turkey. And if you're really ambitious, alligator, bear, and rattlesnake."

Being held in Guy's arms next to Brown, Thelma curiously eyed the man's round face. Then, in childish naivety, she reached out her tiny hand and ran a finger down his scar that went from his sideburn halfway down his cheek.

"Owie," she said in her sweet, childlike voice.

Guy gulped. His eyes rounded, and his brow creased as he looked at Brown in anticipation of some sort of furious reaction.

Instead, Brown took the child's hand, kissed her fingers, and smiled. "Yes, owie," he said, patting her curly head. Thelma smiled.

"Well, what do you think?" asked Guy, trying to distract Brown from Thelma's intrusive behavior.

"We'll consider the property. We're looking at others, but it's certainly within what we're looking for." Brown took one last look at the lake then descended the dike back to the car.

The men were halfway down the path when Guy stopped abruptly and turned around.

"Don't move!" he shouted. He pulled out his pistol, aimed the weapon, and pulled the trigger.

Thelma screamed and slapped her hands over her ears as the sharp, abrupt sound reverberated through the landscape. Blood mixed with flesh rose into the afternoon air then settled onto the path just as Brown's out-of-breath driver bounded toward them, gun drawn. Lying between Guy and Brown was the decapitated carcass of a large diamondback rattlesnake. Guy handed Thelma to Brown, shoved the gun into his waistband, and pulled out a pocket knife. He cut off the rattle, almost four inches long, then kicked the remnants of the dead serpent off the path.

"See what I mean? Protection," said Guy. He wrapped the bloodied rattle in his handkerchief and handed it to Brown. Then he retrieved Thelma, who threw her arms around his neck and whimpered.

"You should come work for me," said Brown. "I could use a man with your acute hearing and aim."

"Thanks for the offer, but I've got enough to do here," said Guy.

The day was turning to dusk when they arrived back at the office.

"Hey, it's getting late. Why don't you fellows come to the house and have dinner before you head back to Miami? Aren't too many restaurants between here and there, and Edna's doesn't serve dinner."

"Thanks," said Brown. "We'll take you up on it."

~

"You touched the face of Al Capone, and Guy saved his life?" asked Leslie, as dumbfounded as the rest of us upon hearing the story.

"At the time, I didn't know Mr. Brown was Al Capone, but from then on, people referred to me as 'the girl who touched the face of Capone,' like he was God or something. When I got older, Uncle Guy told me who he was. After that, I wasn't so proud of what they called me. Yet, to this little girl, he seemed like a nice man even though he'd killed his share of men. Gave me five dollars before he left just cause I was cute. That was a big deal back then."

"Yes, it was. Did Capone ever purchase the land?" Connor asked.

"Naw," said Thelma with a wave of her hand. "Said he found something better closer to Miami."

"Did Guy see Capone again?" I asked.

"That I know of, they only saw each other that one time. But after Uncle Guy had Brown, his driver, and that Giblin fellow for dinner, I understand that Brown, I mean, Capone, said he'd never forget how Guy saved him from the rattler. And he wouldn't forget his kindness in having them for dinner."

"Do you have any more relatives close by?" I wanted to see if we could talk to anyone else while in town.

"I'm the only one still up here in Pahokee. Guy sold the newspaper in 1941 and moved down to Ft. Lauderdale shortly after that. The rest of the clan followed. But I wouldn't try to contact them. They ain't too friendly. That's why I still live up here."

"Thanks for the warning," I said.

"Just one more thing about Uncle Guy," said Thelma. "Did you know he was the first one to get the authorities interested in building Alligator Alley across the state? Course they wanted to name the highway Everglades Parkway, but Alligator Alley won out in the end."

I looked at Leslie. "I didn't know that, did you?"

"One can always learn something new," she said.

"Anything else you want to know?" Thelma gazed at each of us.

"I do have one last question," I said. "Have you ever heard of a man by the name of Derick Eastway?"

Thelma brought her index finger to face and tapped her cheek. "Let me see. Derick Eastway. No. I ain't ever heard of him."

"Well, thank you for your time, Ms. Thelma. You've been very hospitable to us strangers." Leslie rose, collected our glasses, and took them into the kitchen.

"Well, the good book says to be careful to entertain strangers 'cause they just might be angels. Are you angels?" asked Thelma with her toothless grin.

"Maybe," said Connor with a wink.

"Well, come by again if you're ever in the area. My door is always open to angels." Thelma gave us a big toothless smile as she followed us to the door.

Each of us hugged her before leaving. I couldn't imagine how this sweet lady had anything to do with Eastway's death.

"Saving Capone's life is enough for me to see why Guy's name wound up on the key tag," said David, getting into the car.

"If we do find money that belongs to Guy, I'm all for giving it to Thelma," said Leslie.

"Let's not get ahead of ourselves. We have a long way to go even to find out if there's anything still left in the boxes." Connor started the car and pulled away from the curb.

"I agree. Thelma's a lovely lady, but the court will eventually decide who gets the contents," I said.

"I might be able to help you with the banks," said David. "I became friends with a senator on the Banking,

Housing, and Urban Affairs Committee. Maybe he could help us understand what might have happened to the contents of the safe deposit boxes."

"That's a generous offer." Yet, I was still unsure we should let David join our sleuthing group even though he'd helped us thus far.

Then again, maybe allowing him to take the lead on one aspect of the mystery would prove his worth and commitment. Besides, none of us were familiar with the banking industry.

"Yes, please go ahead and pursue that lead. We'd love to know more about what happened to the safe deposit boxes. When we get home, I'll email you a list of the bank names."

"I'll let you know which of them still exist under the original name, which ones went out of business, and which were bought out by another bank, and what the name currently is. I'll also contact the banks still in existence and query them about the disposition of the contents of the safety deposit boxes. There may be a government mandate that governs this. If so, I'll find out what it is as well." David seemed thorough in his approach.

"Great. Connor's friend is still running tests on the keys, so perhaps we'll have further information in a week or so. The four of us can get together then and see what you came up with." This assignment would be a good test for David to see if he was really part of the team.

"I hope I don't have to wait that long to see my wife here," said David with a laugh.

From the front seat, I could tell he was ogling Leslie, maybe even squeezing her hand. I prayed he had good intentions regarding her. I didn't want my precious friend to get hurt.

Chapter 6

The weekend had been fantastic, and the trip productive. Now, I needed to get back to the studio, and Connor still had work to do on the cottage. He wanted to spruce up the place so his parents would have an extended, comfortable stay whenever they came. I figured the Army would phone any day now and want him for a new assignment. Of course, he'd say 'yes,' so I wanted our time together to last as long as possible.

As I got ready for work, nausea and fatigue returned. Then realization came to me like a missile hitting its target—I'd missed a period. Was I pregnant? After all, neither Connor nor I had used protection for over three months. The potential reality hit me hard. Was I ready for this?

Randi get a grip. Get a pregnancy test.

While heading to the studio, I stopped at the drug store. When I got to the office, I went directly to the restroom. Fifteen minutes seemed a long time to sit on the lid of the commode and wait for the results, but it gave me time to absorb the possibility that I may be pregnant. I'd shied away from wanting children, but now that Connor was in my life, I kept looking at the wand, and, in a way, hoping I was. Finally, the answer—positive! My mind became a confused jumble of excitement and dread. How was I going to get through the rest of my busy day?

I sat in my office trying to come to grips with the test results, knowing that I still had work to do and address the ladies getting ready to have their annual quilt show around the corner in the studio. While I'd taped their craft show before Christmas, this would be the first quilt show I'd seen and produced for our YouTube channel. Starting with the show, I'd then video new programs to introduce the art of quilt making to include: quilt patterns, selecting fabric, cutting techniques, and piecing. Each aspect of quilt making would become a segment by itself. When the quilt top was complete, I'd produce a video to show how to finish the quilt—selecting backing and batting, sandwiching the materials, quilting, and binding. The process was arduous, but the results glorious. While mired in all the production details, Adele, my aunt and manager of the fabric store, popped her head into the office.

"Got a few minutes, Randi?"

"Of course. Are the quilts ready to hang?" I asked.

"Most of them are here. That's what I wanted to talk to you about. But first, are you okay? You look a bit pale." Adele walked over and felt my head. "No fever, so that's good."

"I'm okay, just a bit tired. It was a busy weekend." I wasn't about to tell her I was pregnant before informing Connor.

"And, how was your trip to Lake Okeechobee?" Adele took a seat opposite my desk.

"Very pleasant. Everything went well."

"Good to hear. Now, about the quilts, instead of hanging them just in the studio, I'd like to hang some in the store and the reception area of the upholstery shop so people could wander through all the buildings. That would help sales, and things wouldn't get so crowded in here. What do you think?" Adele looked expectantly at me.

"That's a great idea. When do you want to put them up?" I answered robotically. My body seemed to be in the office, but my mind wasn't.

"The standards to display the quilts come tomorrow morning, so that's when we'll start hanging them. I'm sure you'll want to video them, much like the Holiday Bazaar."

"Of course. Come in any time after 8:00 a.m."

"Perfect. See you then."

After Adele left, I knew I needed to refocus. Had Mandy made any genealogical headway finding relatives of the three ladies mentioned in Capone's biography? I put in a call to her, hoping our conversation would take my mind off things.

"Good to hear from you, Randi. Your project has taken me on an interesting ride," said Mandy.

"How so?"

"Well, I've just finished the search for the first lady, Ilsa Carpuchi, and turned up some fascinating stuff. I can give you a brief overview if you like."

"That can wait until I get your report. What I need to know is whether you've found any relatives and their contact info."

"Let me see." I could hear Mandy sorting through some papers. "Oh, here they are. Yes, she has several great-grandchildren scattered throughout the country, but her only living grandchild lives down your way. Her name is Sue Cameron, and she lives in Deerfield Beach at a place called

Century Village. I'll email you her contact information and the report. Then I'll move on to the other women."

"Fabulous. Looks like we're making headway, at least in locating the relatives of some of the people. I'll get in touch with her as soon as possible. And, thanks, Mandy." I was excited to know that the granddaughter lived only a couple of miles away.

In a jiffy, the information on Sue Cameron arrived in my e-mail, and I placed a call to her. Finding her home, I made an appointment to meet her tomorrow at her condo after work. I was sure Leslie would want to join me.

I gave Connor a peck on the cheek when I got home. He was on the patio firing up the grill while Bigfoot antagonized the lizards around the perimeter of the pool.

"Dinner won't be ready for about forty-five minutes if you want to swim a few laps before we eat."

"Great. I'll go change." I started for the house. Swimming always seemed to perk me up emotionally and physically.

"You know what? Dinner can wait. I'll join you in the pool. Who knows what may happen?" Connor turned off the grill.

"After my laps," I said, turning toward him. "I want to keep my girlish figure as long as possible. In a few months, my tummy will be expanding and make me look like the pumpkin you alluded to when you first posed the question about having babies."

Connor did a double-take. "You're pregnant?"

"That's what the test showed." I wasn't sure if I should smile or wince.

I soon found myself twirling around in Connor's arms like his father had done to me when we first met. His kisses landed wherever I had exposed skin. Putting me down, he knelt and lifted my blouse, his lips showering my tummy with kisses.

With his cheek pressed against my abdomen, he pulled me close. "Wow! A little Romero!"

While I was still apprehensive about becoming a mother, loving warmth pulsed through me as I stroked Connor's head, easing my reluctance.

"Hey," I said. "What about our swim?"

"Coming right up, Mrs. Romero and baby."

That night, Connor's goodnight kisses were meant for two.

~

Adele and the ladies arrived at the studio just after 8:00 a.m. The studio was filled with a beehive of activity for most of the day as we put together dozens of quilt display stands. I knew I'd need additional assistance with my morning sickness, so Connor and Archie aided me. They were always Johnny's on the spot when we needed some muscle. By the afternoon, we were exhausted, having hung over thirty-five quilts between the three venues. The quilts were all stunning and would attract customers from far and wide.

Many of the quilts were traditional patterns, while other contemporary landscape quilts depicted sunsets over mountains, winter scenes with trees and snow, farm scenes on rolling hills, and beach scenes with palm trees and crashing waves. We even had small quilts that hung like pictures on a wall with an embroidered vase of flowers, a cardinal perched on a birdhouse, and a row of multi-colored houses on a San Francisco hill. And then there was the large aquarium filled with brain and fan coral, schools of tropical fish in vibrant hues, yellow and red sea horses, and purple and blue jellyfish. Other fascinating and colorful sea creatures peeked from behind rocks. The quilt display was eclectic, one that would appeal to a variety of tastes.

"I'm pooped," I said when we finished in the late afternoon.

I plopped into a chair in the studio and marveled at the display of colorful, eye-popping quilts we'd hung. The exhibit and sale would be a roaring success, by the looks of things.

"Are you sure you've got enough energy to go to Sue Cameron's later?" asked Connor, who hovered over me like a momma bird now that I was pregnant.

"Connor, I'm not going to break. I'm just exhausted."

"Well, I don't want our baby's mom to get too tired." He kissed me on the forehead. "Let's go home, and I'll fix you a nice hot bath. You can soak for a while before you have to run off."

As we rose to lock up the studio, a woman I'd never seen before burst through the door. She rushed over to us out of breath. Her brown hair curled attractively about her oval face, and her makeup, including the muted pink lipstick, had been applied with great care. Her clothes and Mary Jane shoes were out of an expensive Boca boutique.

"Here's my quilt." The middle-aged woman dropped a bulging tote bag at our feet without further explanation.

"I'm sorry, but the quilts are already up. We were just closing." I gestured toward the display.

"Well, you can't close up without my quilt. My work is the star of the show, in more ways than one." She stood there, head erect, eyes and jaw set.

"Have you spoken to Adele? She's the one in charge. We were just..." But before I could finish, Connor broke in.

"Could I ask your name, ma'am?" His tone was calm, friendly.

"Mrs. Jamison. Mrs. Paul Jamison." Her gaze toured us up and down in our grubby work clothes, as though we were the hired help instead of the owners.

"Of course. Jamison Furniture," Connor said.

I looked at him wide-eyed. How would he know the upscale family-owned furniture shop? We hadn't shopped for furniture since he'd been back.

"Yes. Everybody knows of Jamison's," the woman said in a huffy tone. "I just do quilting as a hobby."

"Well, Mrs. Jamison, how about we make an exception for your quilt?" Connor picked up the tote. "Now, don't you worry. We'll put your work in the best spot," he said as he walked Mrs. Jamison to the door.

She left with a smile on her face.

"How could you tell her that? We've already set up the display according to Adele's diagram. We can't cram another quilt in here." As far as I could see, he was meddling where he shouldn't be.

"Look, I'll stay here and put up Mrs. Jamison's quilt. Why don't you go on home and get ready for your appointment?"

"I won't be dismissed that easily," I chided. "Just what do you have in mind?"

"Trust me. I'll make sure her quilt hangs in just the right spot without messing up Adele's lineup. Doing favors for people who don't deserve it can turn out to be a blessing. You'll see." Connor pulled me to him and planted a warm kiss on my lips.

How could I argue with that?

~

The well-known complex known as Century Village made up a small community of about ten thousand people just south of Boca Raton. Several communities in Broward and Palm Beach counties were built in the 1970s, promoted by the Jewish actor and comedian, Red Buttons. The one- and two-bedroom units in two- and three-story condo buildings in Deerfield Beach, occupied mainly by those of the Jewish faith when built, now housed an eclectic mix of residents of all religions and ethnicities.

"One thing about the Century Villages, they know how to take care of their residents. Rides to the grocery store or doctor, an auditorium for plays and events, hobby and card rooms. Residents hardly have to leave the community," said Leslie.

"Have you ever considered moving into a facility like this?" I asked as we pulled up to the entrance. The guard asked for my ID and who I was seeing. After he checked my credentials and his security screen, the gate went up, and we drove into the sprawling complex.

"Sometimes. But I like where I live. Besides, I have the best neighbor." Leslie smiled at me.

"Here it is. Building C, Apartment 212." I parked in a guest spot, and we took the elevator to the second floor.

"You must be Randi Brooks," said Sue Cameron through the screen door. "Come on in. Please forgive my attire. I just came from the workout room." She wore a scooped neck pink sleeveless T-shirt over black tights. A pink terry sweatband wrapped around her forehead and short frosted hair, and she dabbed at the perspiration on her forehead and neck with a small white towel. For someone in her sixties, she looked tanned and toned.

"If this is a bad time, we can come back another day," I said.

"No, no. This is perfect. I'd planned to get back earlier but got caught up in a conversation with another resident and had difficulty pulling away. Can I get you something to drink?" Sue's lithe form moved gracefully into the kitchen.

"Former dancer?" asked Leslie.

"How could you tell?" Sue opened the refrigerator.

"The turned out feet, your graceful arm movements. I could tell," said Leslie.

"Was a Rockette for many years, but at some point, your joints just don't work the way they used to. I retired from dancing years ago, but I still like to work out. Can I get you some water, tea?"

"We're fine," I said. "We just want to ask you a few questions."

"When you called, it sounded so mysterious. I think you said you wanted to know about my grandmother Ilsa Carpuchi. Can you tell me why you're asking about her?" Sue grabbed a bottle of water from the fridge, then moved to the living room and gestured for us to sit. She sat opposite us, crossing her firm legs.

"First, allow me to tell you a little about Leslie and myself. We're what you'd call amateur sleuths. Through our research and inquiries, we've helped the police solve several local crimes."

"Oh? And does your current crime involve my grandmother?" Sue's gaze bounced between Leslie and me as she sipped her water.

"Not exactly," said Leslie. "While we're not at liberty to tell you everything about our investigation, we can tell you that this particular inquiry does involve your grandmother, but not a crime."

"That's a relief, but confusing." Sue sat back, her brow furrowed.

"We understand your grandmother lived in Brooklyn at the same time as the Capone family. We also know that Al was one of her students. What we're looking for is information on your mother's relationship to the young Al Capone." I hoped Sue wouldn't think us too inquisitive.

"Are you writing a book or something?" asked Sue. "It seems odd you'd be asking me about something that happened so long ago. I realize Capone was an interesting person, but..."

I looked at Leslie and gave her a slight nod.

"Without getting into specifics, we're investigating something that may belong to your grandmother or her heirs," Leslie said. "As soon as we can put the pieces together, we'll be glad to give that information to the rightful owners."

"And this has to do with Al Capone?" Sue asked.

Leslie nodded. "That's what we've been led to believe."

"Well, I must tell you, you've come to the right place." Sue gave us a big grin. "My grandmother used to tell me some fantastic stories about her time teaching in Brooklyn. When I was a teen, I wrote down a lot of what she told me. I hoped to organize these remembrances into a book at some point but never did. I still have the stories."

"Do any of them include Al Capone?" I hoped she had at least one that included the head of the Chicago Outfit.

"Yes," said Sue. "Of course, Grandma didn't know the boy she was teaching would turn out to be one of the nation's leading gangsters."

"So, how come she remembered him out of all of her other students?" I asked.

"You'll see when you read the story." Sue got up from her seat and went into a back room.

Leslie and I gave each other thumbs up. A few minutes later, Sue returned with a bound scrapbook filled with loose pages.

"Can we read it here?" Leslie asked.

"Actually, there are only a couple of chapters regarding my grandmother and Al Capone. Let me find them, and I'll make copies. Then you can take them home. Let's move to the table where we can spread out." Sue led us to a small dining table, where she placed the album and began sorting through the pages. After a few minutes, Sue picked up a stack of papers, excused herself, and went into a back room. She emerged with a red folder full of pages.

"Are these the chapters?" asked Leslie.

"I believe these are the only ones that you'll need. I certainly hope they help you figure out what belongs to my grandmother."

"I assure you we will be in contact as soon as we finish our investigation." I handed Sue my business card and tucked the folder into my bag. "By the way, since you live in Deerfield Beach, have you ever run across a man by the name of Derick Eastway?"

"Does he live in Century Village, too?" Sue asked.

"No, he lives just off the ocean on the east side of town," I replied.

"Sorry, I mostly stay on this side and don't go east much. I've never met him."

"Well, thanks for your time," I said as Leslie and I left.

"Isn't this exciting?" asked Leslie as we made our way to the car.

"Without a doubt. I'll go through the papers tonight and fill you in tomorrow. By the way, what's happening with you and David?"

"Oh, we still talk but haven't seen each other since the weekend."

I couldn't tell if she was happy or sad about that.

"Well, sometimes letting love bloom slowly is the better way to go." I pulled onto SW 18th Street, welcoming less traffic than traveling up Military Trail.

"Advice from a young woman with a long life ahead of her."

"I'm just saying there's no rush. David's a nice guy, but you don't know him yet. Give the relationship time."

"Tootsie, when you're my age, you don't know how much time you have. Sometimes, you just have to seize the moment."

"What are you saying? That you want a relationship with David? Want to live together? Get married?" I was confused. Leslie always struck me as being so independent she'd never consider another relationship after her husband died.

"All I'm saying is maybe you and Connor could come over sometime and make some suggestions on how I could reorganize my boxes."

Connor would be as ecstatic as I was to hear she was ready for both house cleaning and a relationship.

"You know we'll help you. Connor and I are great organizers." I smiled as I turned into our neighborhood.

"Enough said. Let me know what you find out about Sue's grandmother." Leslie got out in front of her house and threw me a kiss before heading down the sidewalk.

I went home to curl up in bed with Bigfoot and read Sue's writings. Hopefully, they would shed some light on why her grandmother's name was on one of Capone's key tags.

Chapter 7

"How'd the quilt hanging go? Where'd you put Mrs. Jamison's quilt?" I asked Connor when he came into the bedroom that night.

"You'll have to wait until tomorrow. Don't want to give away the surprise." He gave me his trademark wink and grin as he undressed and slid under the sheets to accompany me. He'd brought a trade magazine on the latest investigative techniques to read. Bigfoot snuggled between us.

"I know what that means. You've got something up your sleeve. Well, I hope you made sure what you did won't embarrass Adele, the other ladies, or Mrs. Jamison. When I phoned Adele to tell her what happened, she told me Mrs. Jamison is always late, but she didn't think she'd show up *after* we'd finished putting up the display. She also said Jamison's Furniture does a lot of business with us, so I don't want to jeopardize that relationship. I already did that one time with the Wellingtons and Mr. Montague remember? I don't want to go through another fiasco like that."

"Don't worry. I handled the situation in a most delicate way. I'd never put the company's reputation in a compromising position."

Connor's thumbing through his magazine in such an unconcerned fashion didn't soothe my mind. I'd only become more curious to know what exactly he'd done to appease Mrs. Jamison while supporting the quilt show. All I could do at the moment was concentrate on reading Sue's writings and leave Mrs. Jamison's quilt until tomorrow. The whole thing left me with an uneasy feeling.

The papers Sue gave me turned out to be a combination of her writings and pages from a journal her grandmother wrote. I had to piece the dates and times together to get the whole picture, but once I had them in their proper order, I was able to see why Ilsa Carpuchi would remember one boy out of hundreds she'd taught over the years.

~

New York 1912

Theresa Capone stood in the open doorway of the derelict building—doors off their hinges, broken windows, stairs falling down—and peeked around the corner. There he was. Not yet noon, a time when he should be in school, instead, Alfonso was down on his knees playing craps with three other youth from the neighborhood. Whoops and hollers rose from the boys as they tossed the dice against the wall, oblivious to Theresa's hard stare behind them.

She had traipsed down the block with her head up, determination in her eyes, and fury in her soul. Wearing her day clothes covered by a flowered apron, she headed toward the abandoned building she'd been told about after she received a note from her son's school. Alfonso had missed dozens of days in the last month when she believed he was neatly tucked behind his desk at PS 133. Before the family's move to South Brooklyn, Al had maintained a B average. He was a bright kid with lots of potential. She hoped he'd be the first in the family to graduate from high school. Now he was close to flunking out.

Mustering the courage she'd arrived with and careful not to fall through the holes in the floor, Thersa stormed into the room. She grabbed Alfonso by the ear lobe, lifting him from the floor.

"How could you? We're going home. If you boys know what's good for you, you'll head that way, too." Red-faced, Theresa spouted the emphatic and demanding message to her son and the other boys in Italian as her English had not progressed far.

Al, thirteen, tried wriggling from his mother's grasp, all to no avail. Aside from losing his dignity, he left his dice and earnings behind as Theresa hauled him back through the falling-down building. The other boys laughed and smirked as he left, yet their time for similar discipline was just minutes away. As soon as Theresa marched her son the block back home, the whole South Brooklyn neighborhood would be ripe with gossip. When informed of their sons' escapade, the other boy's parents would be as livid as Theresa.

When she got to their home, Theresa followed Al up the stairs and into their apartment. The door closed with emphasis after them.

"What's wrong with you, Alfonso?" Theresa asked in her loud, expressive Italian tongue. She knew the neighbors could hear. "Your father and I came here to give you every opportunity to get a good education and improve yourself. Yet, all you've done is squander this away." She looked at her son, a scowl on her face.

"I hate school," Al spat.

The embarrassment of being dragged home by his ear added to this loathing, culminating in uncontrolled anger. He picked up a blue and white plate from the counter and slammed it to the floor. Shards of china shot haphazardly along the linoleum. He had exhibited an angry streak ever since he was a small child and hated people telling him what to do. Most of the time, he'd been able to control his rage, but lately, his temper had gotten shorter and more volatile.

"No wonder. You've missed thirty-three days out of the last ninety school days. Your grades are failing, and you'll have to repeat sixth grade if you miss any more. Your father will be most disappointed when he hears of this. Tomorrow, he and I will accompany you to meet with your principal. Clean up this plate, then go to your room and think this over." Theresa pulled the broom and dustpan from the pantry and held them toward Al.

His face flushed with anger as he ignored his mother's directive and stomped off to his room. "I'll quit school, and they'll be nothing you can do about it," he yelled over his shoulder.

Theresa shook her head, then swept up the broken plate.

By the following morning, Alfonso was a humbled thirteen-year-old as he accompanied his father, Gabriel, and his mother, Theresa, to William A. Butler school. Sandwiched between his parents as they sat in Mr. Agosti's office, Al listened to the principal speak of the dire circumstances surrounding his failing grades because he missed so much school. In the end, Al promised to quit playing hooky and attend classes.

His promise lasted the next two weeks, even though he'd have preferred playing stickball in the street, craps in the alley, or pool in the hall down the block. He brought his dice to school every day, feeling sure he could convince some of the boys to play craps at recess. He'd be gambling with his future, but Al didn't care. School was not for him.

"What's that you have?" asked Mrs. Ilsa Carpuchi, Al's teacher.

"Nothing," he said, slipping the dice into his pants pocket.

"Come here. Let me see."

Al reluctantly rose. Smirking, he took his time shuffling through the desks to the front of the class. His classmates snickered behind him. They knew he had stepped into the thick sticky pile of dodo with both feet.

Mrs. Capuchi stuck out her hand. "Give them to me," she said, in no uncertain terms.

Al dug into his pocket, pulled out the white ivory cubes with black pips, and dropped them into Mrs. Capuchi's palm. She held them up for all Al's classmates to see.

"This is what's been keeping Al from school and his grades dropping, boys and girls. He's a bright boy, but he'll never get ahead or make anything of himself if he keeps letting things like this distract him from his education. I hope this is a good lesson for all of you."

Suddenly, Al slapped Mrs. Capuchi's hand, sending the dice tumbling to the floor. Mrs. Capuchi stood there, mouth agape and eyes wide in surprise. Everyone in the classroom gasped, shocked by Al's brazen act of defiance. Al bent down, scooped up the dice, and made for the door. When he got there, he ran directly into Mr. Agosti, who had come down to see how Al was getting along.

"What's your hurry?" Mr. Agosti asked, grabbing the boy by his shirt collar.

Though Al struggled, Mr. Agosti held tight as he escorted him back into the classroom. He saw the students in an uproar and tears in Mrs. Capuchi's eyes.

"He needs disciplining," said Mrs. Capuchi. She explained what had transpired.

Mr. Agosti marched Al right out of the classroom into his office and gave Al a good whipping.

That was the last time Al showed his face at PS 133. From then on, he hung out around various venues in the neighborhood, joined a youth gang, and held a job for a short time now and then until his temper got the best of him. Then he moved on to something new.

~

"Good grief," I uttered, forgetting Connor was in bed next to me. Having fallen asleep, he jerked awake at my exclamation. So did Bigfoot.

"What?" he asked, sitting up. The open trade magazine on his lap slid to the floor.

"I now know why Ilsa Carpuchi was on the safe deposit tag."

"Why?" asked Connor, blinking.

"Al slapped her when she scolded him in front of her students for squandering his opportunity for an education."

"So, he rewarded her for embarrassing him in front of his peers by putting money into a safety deposit box in her name? That doesn't make sense."

"No. I think it was more like Al was remorseful for having slapped her. That's why he included her name on one of the tags. She was someone he'd remember," I said.

"Don't forget, Capone didn't plan to give any of the money away. The cash was supposed to be used for his retirement after he got out of Alcatraz."

"Then I guess we'll never really know why he used her name or any of the others. We can only speculate."

75

Connor yawned, turned over, and nestled under the covers. Bigfoot closed his eyes and went back to sleep, too.

Not me. I was left wide awake trying to figure out the mystery of Capone's keys and what they had to do with Derick Eastway's death.

~

Connor poured me a mug-to-go of coffee and set it on the kitchen island. "Heading out?" He kissed my cheek.

"I can't wait to see how you solved the problem of Mrs. Jamison's quilt. I realize, of course, you'll be staying here and working on the cottage. How convenient. If there is a problem at the studio, you'll be nowhere around. I guess that means I'll have to handle the fallout." I grabbed a dark cherry yogurt from the fridge.

"You have no faith in your husband," Connor said.

"Not so, mon cher. I do have faith in you, but I also know you can be a bit of a jokester." I arched my brows and gave him a stare.

Connor laughed. "We'll talk about it when you get home."

"I'm sure we will." I gave him a big smooch, grabbed my coffee, and headed for the door. I was a bit apprehensive driving to the studio, but I tried to keep my optimism at its peak by smiling and turning on some country music.

I pushed the code into the digital lock on the studio door and paused, taking a deep breath before entering. When I turned on the light, I scanned the room. Not seeing Mrs. Jamison's quilt, I walked through each row of the displayed quilts. Still nothing. My heart began to pound, and my mouth went dry. Connor had to have hung the quilt somewhere. I didn't want to call him and give him the satisfaction of telling me where it was. I was a sleuth, wasn't I? I should be able to figure that out.

Walking around the studio, I finally saw the quilt reflected in the glass window that divided the studio from the production room. I tilted my head back. A canopy of stars and exploding galaxies in dazzling colors swirled above my head as though they were part of the divine celestial universe. How Connor had hung the quilt there was a marvel and oh so clever. Kind of like a big secret awaiting discovery. I could hardly wait to see how many guests noticed the quilt and their reaction. And, of course, how Mrs. Jamison would respond. She couldn't deny that her masterpiece had been displayed in grand fashion.

"Thought I'd find you here," said Archie. "Everything looks great. How are you feeling these days?"

"Some days better than others."

"Well, you look very content, not just about being pregnant but about the quilt show as well. Looking forward to today?"

"Of course. I'm ready to video the show and talk to the guests. It's always so exciting to see us do something new. What about you? How's your role as Archie Confessor going?"

"Not bad, but I got a call the other day that disturbed me. I was hoping we could talk about it."

"I can't imagine I could say anything to the person who called that would come even close to the advice you could give."

"Advice isn't what this person was looking for, Miss Randi." Archie's eyebrows knitted together, and he dropped his head.

"Then what?" I asked. But before Archie could tell me, Adele and her ladies entered the studio, all chatting away.

"We can talk later, Miss Randi." Archie turned to go.

"Probably best. I've got to get my camera rolling."

Archie left for the upholstery shop, and I started taping.

"We're here," Adele called. She led her entourage into the studio, where they settled behind the welcome table and organized their cash box, tickets, and other paraphernalia. They had hardly been there fifteen minutes when the first guest arrived.

I hadn't recorded much when I heard someone behind me.

"Excuse me."

I switched off my camera and turned toward the voice.

"Oh, hi, Mrs. Jamison. How are you enjoying the show?"

"Is that nice young handyman here? The one I spoke with yesterday?"

"You mean my husband, Connor Romero?"

"He's your husband?"

I held up my left hand, showing her my wedding ring. "He's at home. Can I help you with something?"

"Please tell him I'm thrilled with how he hung my quilt. It does the design justice to be hanging as though we're looking at the midnight sky. When I designed the quilt to depict the heavens and an exploding galaxy, I had no idea the image would look so natural floating above us."

"I'll be sure to tell him. He'll be delighted to know you approve."

"And please pass on to the owner of the business my sincere delight with the exhibit."

"You just did," I said.

Mrs. Jamison did a doubletake. "You?"

I nodded. "The business has been in my family since the 1960s. After my parents died last year, I inherited the fabric store and upholstery shop then added the studio. I'm Randi Brooks." I would have extended my hand, but I was still holding the camera.

"Oh, yes. I remember reading about it—my sincere condolences. Well, I shouldn't keep you from your work. Please present my card at Jamison's if you ever need any furniture. They'll treat you especially nice." She withdrew a Jamison's Furniture business card with her name and handed it to me.

"Thank you," I said, looking at the card. I doubted I'd ever use it. Still, it was a nice gesture.

I taped customers' reactions to the display for the rest of the day. Everyone seemed pleased with the variety of quilts and was especially fond of the aquarium. Some stood for the longest time mesmerized by all the colorful creatures tucked behind the rocks and corals.

I shut off the camera at five o'clock and headed home. When I couldn't find Connor in the house, I wandered out to the patio. Sure enough, I found him stretched out in a lounge chair. I dropped into the chaise next to him, glad to be off my feet.

"How'd it go with Mrs. Jamison?" he asked.

"She loved what you did with her quilt. I married a very clever man." I leaned over and gave him a big kiss.

"Was that ever in question?" The corners of his mouth turned up into a sly, sexy smile.

"Not for a moment," I said. "So, who's cooking tonight?"

"I've got chicken marinating in the refrigerator. Dinner will be in about forty minutes."

"Great. I need to go over to Leslie's and tell her about Ilsa Carpuchi." I rose from the lounge and started across the patio.

"Okay, but don't be late for dinner," Connor called after me.

"What if I am?" I teased.

"They'll be consequences."

I laughed as I slipped through the secret gate in the hedge and crossed to Leslie's back door. I was tempted to be late just to find out what those consequences were.

Chapter 8

Connor and I had an appointment with Dr. Nina Morrow for a checkup and ultrasound, now that ten weeks had passed. As we left the office, we were ecstatic everything was going well with the pregnancy, but we were also stunned by the results—twins!

"Well, that was quite the surprise, especially for someone reluctant to have children in the first place." I gripped Connor's hand as though I were hanging on for dear life. Maybe I was.

He let go of my hand, put his arm around my shoulders, and pulled me to him.

"Mrs. Romero, you're not alone in this. Marriage and parenthood is a partnership, remember? We'll do just fine." Confidence oozed from Connor's composure.

We wouldn't know for another few weeks what the genders were, but that wouldn't matter. Whether they were identical, fraternal, boys, girls, or one of each, they would be loved unconditionally. The time was right to tell family and friends.

After informing the Romeros, we told Leslie, Rachel, and the staff at A Stitch in Time. Everyone was thrilled for us and couldn't wait to hear about the gender of the babies. We wanted to know, too, to plan the babies' room.

I spent the next few days at the studio videotaping and working on the mystery of Capone's keys. Mandy called on Friday and gave me an update on the other two women whose names we found on the key tags. She followed up with an email containing additional information. The next name on my list was Lena Galluccio. Mandy said she found a recording in the National Archives from Billie Badami, researcher and author. The recording was of his recollections of an interview with Frank Galluccio, the man who gave Capone his scars. She forwarded a link to the recording. Lena Galluccio had to be related to Frank, though I didn't know how—sister, wife, mother, cousin? I was sure the recording would clear things up.

Leslie came over after dinner. She, Connor, and I sat in the sunroom as I clicked on the link so we could listen to the recording. While this wouldn't solve the question of what was in her safe deposit box, David was still investigating that, the recording would give us insight into why Lena's name was on the key tag.

~

New York 1918
    The Harvard Inn, a dive of a dance hall and bar— dark, dingy, crowded, loud—was owned by local hoodlum, John Torrio, and managed by second in command Frankie Yale, a savvy gang manager in Torrio's organization. The establishment sat at 14 Seaside Walk on Coney Island.

Tonight, as on most nights, the tavern bustled with local patrons out for a good time of music, drinks, and a dance or two. Al Capone, who had been a Yale junior gang member and caught the boss's eye, just turned eighteen. He was now old enough to work in the Inn and had been hired to serve drinks and act as a part-time bouncer when needed. He wore a broad smile as he snaked his way through the crowded tables with his serving tray.

"What'll youse have?" Al had to yell over the loud music and chatter of patrons to get the order of the couples sitting at the four-top.

"Two high balls and two gin fizz," called the pimple-faced male across the table.

Al didn't think the kid was old enough to be there, but he wasn't going to make waves. The age of the customer was none of his concern. His job was to serve drinks and pick up the cash. If he had to put on his bouncer hat, he did so with finesse. The trick, he'd learned from Yale, was to bounce the customer without alienating him. And that was only after failed efforts to quiet the customer and defuse the situation. The Inn wanted the customer and his money, just not his attitude or drunken state.

Strolling down Stratton's Walk toward the Harvard Inn was Frank Galluccio, a former merchant seaman turned hood in the Genovese crime family. Holding onto Frank's arm to steady his gait after their visit to another Coney Island bar was Maria Tanzio, Frank's girlfriend. Tagging along beside them was Frank's kid sister, Lena. They spotted a couple just leaving as they stepped into the Harvard Inn.

"Grab that table," said Frank. Though dirty glasses and spilled drinks lingered on the table's wooden surface, Maria and Lena made a beeline for it.

Spotting the trio, Al hurried over. He'd noticed Lena immediately. She was his type—adequate upfront with a chasse that sent his male hormones surging. As he cleared and wiped the table, his eyes undressed Lena. Recognizing the unwelcomed advance, she turned away. With her nose in the air, she was hoping he'd get the message.

"What can I get ya?" asked Al, his hungry gaze still on Lena.

In his inebriated state, Frank was oblivious to Al's overt display. He waggled his finger between him and Maria and answered, "We'll take two beers. She'll take a ginger ale." Frank pointed to Lena.

Al laughed to himself. "Coming right up."

"Wanta dance?" Frank rose unsteadily and put out his hand toward Marie.

"Sure, honey," she replied, placing her hand in his. They moved onto the dance floor for a slow waltz. A couple of minutes later, Al returned with the drinks.

Lena was uncomfortable sitting there by herself. She dropped her eyes to her hands in her lap. Maybe if she didn't look at him, the jerk would leave her alone.

"I'll bet there's something really nice under those hands," said Al, setting the drinks on the table. A smug grin covered his lips.

Lena's cheeks turned hot. "Beat it," she said with as much courage as she could muster.

Al laughed, then turned to go.

Just then, Frank and Marie returned to the table. A scowl covered Lena's face. "You know that guy?" Frank asked, his words slurred.

"Never saw him before," Lena said. "But he's got some nerve. He's been rude and suggestive. Could you maybe speak to him, Frank? Ask him to stop, but in a nice way?" Lena was well aware her brother took care of others

84

more forcefully, but she didn't want to make a scene. Just a pleasant, "Hey, she's my kid sister. How about leaving her alone?" was all she wanted.

Al headed their way. Now was Frank's opportunity. But before he could get a word out, Al leaned over and spoke to Lena loud enough to unnerve folks at the adjacent table.

"You got a nice ass, honey, and I mean that as a compliment. Believe me."

Frank shot from his seat. "Nobody speaks to my sister like that. Apologize to her," Frank shouted. That some waiter had spoken to his kid sister like that was bad enough, but to be loud enough for other customers to hear? That was unforgivable.

Al was aware he'd crossed the line. Smiling, he spoke in an offhanded yet apologetic tone. "I didn't mean nothin' by it, pal. It was a little misunderstanding, that's all. A joke."

"That wasn't no joke." Frank's tone, flushed face, and clenched fists challenged Al.

At only five-foot-six and weighing under one hundred fifty pounds, Frank knew he was no match for Al's size and weight. Frank dug into his pocket, realizing he'd need an offense other than his fists.

Before Al could react, a switchblade emerged. With the swiftness of an experienced slicer, Frank carved Capone's cheek twice and neck once; blood poured from the open wounds. Al grabbed some cocktail napkins from the table and pressed them against his face and neck, hoping he could stop the bleeding.

Realizing what he'd done and not wasting any time, Frank grabbed Marie and Lena and ran out of the Inn. Another bartender carted Al to the Coney Island hospital, where doctors took thirty stitches to sew up his slashes.

Frank caught rumors that some ruffian from Yale's outfit asked about him a few days later. Knowing the situation was about to explode, he petitioned Joseph Masseria, overlord of New York's crime gangs, to intervene. "Joe the Boss" ordered a sit-down at the Harvard Inn where representatives for Frank and Al met and came to an agreement. Al had been wrong and would not retaliate against Frank. Frank would apologize to Al for his excessive reaction, for which he was genuinely remorseful after seeing Al's scared face.

People soon referred to Al as Scarface. To show the depth of his remorse at the entire incident, when Al became Chicago's kingpin, he hired Frank as a spare bodyguard for $100 a week whenever he was in New York.

~

Leslie, Connor, and I were mesmerized by the recording and sat there for a moment without saying a word.

"Well, that's why Capone included Lena's name on the key tag. She was the one who got away." Connor got up.

"And why he never forgot her," said Leslie, rising to go home. "She stayed with him the rest of his life. Literally."

"Well, we've now figured out three of the names. There's only one more we can readily identify, Eleanor Patterson. I think we'll wait another day or two before we go into her background. The quilt show doesn't end until Saturday, and I need to tape it, so I'll be tied up until then." I rose and walked Leslie to the door. "Have you heard anything from David?"

"He says he's making headway on the banks, but the worst thing about researching anything in Washington is the time it takes to get the information back."

"Don't I know. I spent ten years in that quagmire. Well, let us know when David is ready for us, and he can tell us the results of his research. We'll all go out to eat somewhere."

"What's the matter? Don't you like my cooking?" Connor's tone indicated we'd slighted him.

"You know I do," I said, giving him a peck on the check. "I just supposed a nice thing to do was give the cook the night off."

"Well, goodnight, you two. We're making headway. And congratulations, again, on your pregnancy. I can't wait to hold the precious babies." Leslie gave each of us a hug and crossed the patio back to her home.

"Has your buddy gotten back to you about the keys?" I picked up the empty tea mugs and plates from our get-together and took them into the kitchen. He followed.

"Only that he got the package you sent. But I think you might have made a miscalculation on the number of keys. He says he received twelve, and you've got six. That means one is missing from the original nineteen."

"How can that be?" I said, scrunching my face. "I remember counting all of them carefully and putting them into the lockbox. Later I only took out the ones we couldn't read and sent them to Curtis. The ones we could read remained in the box."

"Perhaps you need to recount them. Or better yet, look at your list. Curtis sent me the numbers of the ones he has. We can compare them to what you have and see which one is missing."

I went to my computer and accessed the list. We compared my list to the one Curtis sent.

"Look here," I said. "The number nine key is missing and should have gone to Curtis as it was one of those we couldn't read. He should have had thirteen keys, not twelve. Let me get the lockbox. Maybe the key is in there." I hurriedly retrieved the box from the locked drawer in the file cabinet. Inside, only six keys remained.

"So there is one missing," confirmed Connor.

"This is crazy." My brow furrowed. "I scooped all the keys into the box after we bagged them and later took out the ones I sent to Curtis. I must have made a mistake counting them, but then where is key number nine?"

"Let's look through the kitchen drawers," suggested Connor.

The two of us went through every drawer in the kitchen, pulling out dish clothes, cooking utensils, plastic wrap, and other kitchen paraphernalia. No baggie with the number nine key appeared.

"Don't get too upset about this, honey. You have the rest of the keys. Maybe number nine is one of those you'll never be able to read. Let's wait until Curtis gets back to us to see if he's had any success with the others. Besides, we need to see what David says about the banks. If we can't get into the boxes or their contents have been moved or lost, none of this will make any difference anyway."

"You're right, of course, but I've always prided myself in being organized. Not having that key will haunt me, even if nothing comes of the mystery."

"Come on, Mrs. Romero. Let's go to bed. Whether you solve the mystery or not isn't what's important right now. What's important is that the mother of our twins gets her rest." Connor picked up the lockbox, put an arm around my shoulders, and led me to the stairs. "I'll put the box away; you go ahead on up. I'll be right there."

Despite Connor's reasoning and trying to soothe my ruffled feathers for misplacing the key, I couldn't help but wonder if key number nine would turn out to be the one piece of evidence that brought the whole puzzle together.

Chapter 9

The following two days of the quilt show were busier than ever. By the time the show closed on Saturday, almost all of the quilts for sale had sold. The Palm Beach Planetarium purchased Mrs. Jamison's quilt. She was thrilled to think her handiwork would be on display and appreciated by both children and adults. As I'd neglected the rest of the business while the exhibit and sale took place, I decided to visit Archie before the shop closed. Besides, I owed him a conversation. I found him in his office. We sat in the chairs in front of his desk.

"Looks like Randall needs skates, the way he has to rush around the upholstery shop." It was nice to finally sit down.

"The studio's brought a whole new dimension to A Stitch in Time," said Archie. "Whenever you hold an event, we get so busy we can hardly handle all the business. I'm sure the fabric store is experiencing the same."

"Well, that's why I started the studio. And you, along with Randall, have become internet stars." I smiled, remembering his reluctance even to be part of the DIY projects. Now he and his son Randall had a robust following.

"I'm humbled, Miss Randi. God has blessed all of us."

"He has indeed. Anything else we need to talk about before I go home and collapse? You and Randall have your next upholstery project all set, don't you?"

"We're ready," he said.

"Good. Then I'll see you in the studio in two weeks. What are you going to reupholster this time?"

"A headboard. We're going to take the same headboard and give the audience options on how to take it from plain to wow!"

"Sounds interesting. Can't wait to see how you'll do that." Archie and I hugged before I left.

Driving home, I marveled about how the addition of the studio had enhanced the business at A Stitch in Time and our lives. If not for Leo Barlos and his indiscretion decades ago, we'd still be operating with only two components—the fabric store and upholstery shop. With his gifting me the property out of guilt and my building the studio, now we could offer our goods and services to a broader community.

Of course, I still needed to tell Connor the truth about Leo—that he was my biological father and the twins' grandfather. I'd conveniently neglected to discuss the topic and stuck it into the recesses of my mind, hoping the subject would go away. But with my pregnancy, now was time to tell him and discuss how to handle the issue when the babies arrived. For heaven's sake, they would grow up in the same community as the man. At some point, they'd probably meet him, or at minimum, know who he was. Was their relation to Leo something we'd keep from them? What a mess! Tonight I needed to talk with Connor.

~

A welcomed rain shower came through Boca while Connor and I ate, so instead of going out onto the patio after dinner, we sat at the kitchen island. Then we moved to the sunroom, where I served coffee and dessert.

"You were rather quiet at dinner. Something on your mind?" Connor sat opposite me in a side chair. I sat on the couch; Bigfoot curled beside me.

"Actually, yes," I said, biting my lip. "Though I wish I didn't need to have this conversation."

"Uh-oh. Sounds ominous. Shall I get the tissues?" Connor gazed at me with concern.

"Probably," I said.

Connor grabbed the box and set the tissues on the coffee table. He plucked one out, laid it in my lap, and then sat next to me. Taking my hands in his, warmth and strength pulsed through me, giving me courage. "Whatever the issue, we face it together, Mrs. Romero." Connor's gaze was one of unconditional love.

"Leo Barlos is my biological father." I withdrew my hands from Connor's and took the tissue. Tears spilled from my eyes.

"I figured that but wanted you to tell me in your own time. This is a deeply personal matter, and I didn't want to intrude."

"I love you for that, Connor. But didn't the fact that he's my biological father bother you? Even though you understood what a wicked person he is, you still wanted to marry me?"

"I didn't marry Leo Barlos," said Connor with a laugh. "I married *you*, Randi, the person your parents raised to become a beautiful, accomplished, passionate woman."

"So, you're okay with my genealogical history?"

"We can't change the past. I think the more important question is, how do *you* feel about your family tree?"

"I pretty much came to terms with the reality of Leo's parenthood while I was in D.C., yet now that I'm back and occasionally run into him, I'm conflicted about how to react to him and what to do about the relationship."

"I'm sure that hasn't been easy," said Connor.

"Plus, now that I'm pregnant, he's also the twins' biological grandfather. I'd love for the children to have a close relationship with their grandparents, but I just can't see him being a part of their lives. To have forced himself on my mother right before her wedding to my father was unconscionable. Then there's what he's done to others, including us. To know that he's hurt so many people and never taken responsibility for his actions is so foreign to our values. I've forgiven him for all the pain he's caused me, but I don't plan to embrace him." I dabbed at the tears running down my cheeks.

"Does he know you're pregnant?"

"I haven't told him. So, unless someone else did, he'd have no clue."

"He's going to find out sooner or later. Once you start showing, everyone will know, and we don't want him thinking he can just barge in and be part of our lives. Maybe he won't even care to be involved. Then again, maybe he might. I'm sure he wouldn't want the truth to come out, but it would have to if he tries anything. First, we need to understand our legal rights and his. After we know what we're up against, we'll have a little sit-down."

"Can we think about this for a few days?" I didn't want to make a hasty decision.

"Of course." Connor put his arms around me and pulled me close. "I love you from the depths of my soul, Randi. Let's get the attorney's opinion, have a discussion, and agree on an approach. Then we'll go see Leo together." He kissed me tenderly.

I prayed this situation would have a positive outcome, but I couldn't see how.

~

I spent the first two days of the week editing the videos on the Quilt Exhibit and reading the information I got from Mandy regarding our fourth name on the key tag— Eleanor Patterson. On Tuesday, Connor visited our attorney to inquire about our rights. That night, we drove to the Deerfield Beach pier, where he'd tell me what the lawyer said.

The night was cool to us Floridians—just below seventy degrees—but the temperature was delightful to those northerners down for a winter respite. Connor and I wore light jackets as we paid our entrance fee and walked, hand in hand, down the almost one thousand-foot pier. Periodic lights shone on the wooden walkway and lighted areas where people were fishing.

"I haven't walked the pier in years. What a great place to stroll and talk." The incoming sea breeze brushed the hair from my face.

"As long as you don't mind the smell of fish and all that goes along with catching them." Connor signaled with his head at a man who was gutting a fish.

"It's not that bad. The ocean breeze pretty much washes the odor away. I'll have you know that Dad and Mom brought me to the pier many times in my childhood to fish. We didn't catch much, but I loved talking to the fishermen. We even shrimped several times."

"I like eating shrimp but never caught any. How does that work?"

"Well, you've got to use a lantern that you hang over the water off the pier or a boat to attract the shrimp as they travel in long lines. Then you use a pole with a net attached. When you see the shrimp, you scoop them into the net. But you have to know just how to do that. The shrimp are very cagy and can jump out of the way, so you kind of have to lead them. We used to catch so many we'd fill our gallon bucket. What we didn't eat right away, we froze. We had shrimp for months."

"I keep learning new things about you all the time. How did you get so interesting, Mrs. Romero?" Connor pulled me close.

"Do you realize we've known each other only a year? How could you learn everything about me in that short time? Even a lifetime is too short."

"I love going to different venues and letting you unwrap your experiences." Connor kissed my forehead.

"So, Mr. Romero, what did you find out today?" We stopped at the end of the pier and looked out at the dark, rolling ocean.

"Fortunately, the legal system is on our side. A new law that took effect in 2015 narrowed the circumstances under which a grandparent can sue for visitation rights. Unless we die, one of us becomes single and is convicted of a felony or an offense that poses a threat or harm to the minor child's health or welfare, a grandparent can't sue for visitation. Florida is very protective of the rights of its citizens and makes visitation very difficult to obtain."

"Does this mean we're off the hook as far as Leo is concerned?" I placed my forearms on the railing and peered out at the boat lights traversing the ocean in the distance. Connor did the same.

"Legally, yes. But we have no idea what his reaction will be when he finds out he'll soon be the grandfather of the twins. We need to let him know we're aware of the law. We need to go see him knowing what we want to say and accomplish."

"That's going to require some thought. I don't want to be mean, and we have to think about what would be best for the children in the long term."

"I'm sure between our discussing the issue and prayer, we'll come up with the right answer."

"Sounds like a plan." I turned to Connor. "I'll bet you never considered that marrying me would be so complicated."

Connor put his arms around my waist; I put mine around his neck.

"That's what endeared me to you in the first place. You're like the mysteries I dealt with in my job. Always something new to discover."

"And you like solving mysteries?"

"I like solving your mysteries." He drew me to him and gave me a deep kiss.

As we walked back down the pier, a boy about ten was casting a line into the water. No adult appeared close by.

"How's the fishing?" Connor asked.

"Not much going on tonight, but I've been here when we've caught lots of fish." The boy yanked on his rod, then let the pole settle.

"Come here often?" I asked. He looked well set up with a tackle box, bucket filled with water, and two poles.

"Only when grandpa brings me. He wasn't in one of his meetings tonight, so we were able to come."

"Doesn't he fish with you?" I gazed down the pier for someone who looked like he belonged to the boy. All I saw were other fishermen spaced out farther down the dock.

"He's getting more bait. He should be back in a minute."

Connor and I stood by the boy and looked out onto the water.

"Well, how about that? Randi Brooks and her new husband."

Connor and I turned to find Leo Barlos walking toward us.

"I didn't know you fished," I said with a thick tongue, not knowing what else to say. All I'd seen Leo wear were expensive suits. To see him in jeans, a casual shirt, and a jacket was decidedly different. He looked...normal.

"What? You think I only deal in real estate?" He let out a deep laugh. "This is my grandson Jimmy. Jimmy, this is Mr. and Mrs...I'm sorry, Randi, I don't know your married name."

"Romero. Mr. and Mrs. Connor Romero," said Connor in a no-nonsense tone.

"Nice to meet you," said Jimmy.

"How's everything at the studio?" asked Leo.

I couldn't tell if he was genuinely interested or looking for a sign of failure. With him, I never knew.

"Going well. Your sponsorship certainly helped us get off the ground. How's Boca Bounty? You still have her, don't you?" Boca Bounty was the greyhound Leo owned and raced at the Palm Beach Kennel Club. When the track closed down, he adopted the dog from Greyhound Rescue and Rehabilitation, the charity we supported.

"Doing fine. Jimmy's taken a real shine to her."

"She's a great dog," Jimmy said with a wide smile. "Granddad told me he adopted her at an event you had at your studio. Maybe I could join your group and help out with the dogs."

"Quite possibly. You'll need to speak with Mrs. Cohen. She organizes that part of the programming." I pulled a card from my bag and handed it to Jimmy. "If you're really interested, you can give her a call. Tell her I encouraged you to do so."

"Gosh, thanks," said Jimmy. He beamed as he looked at the card.

"Well, we don't want to keep you from quality time with your grandson," Connor said to Leo.

"Can't keep me from that. Grandparents need to spend as much time as they can with their grandchildren. Don't you agree?" Leo gave us a broad smile and piercing look as he put an arm around Jimmy's shoulders and pulled him close.

I was speechless. All I could do was give a slight nod.

"Come on, honey. Jimmy's got a lot of fishing to do." Connor guided me toward the pier exit as confusion swirled in my head.

"Did you hear what he said? See that look? Do you think he knows?" I asked.

"Naw. I think Leo was just expressing a commonly held belief. Even we believe that grandparents should spend time with their grandchildren," Connor soothed.

"I know, but don't you think it's odd that we'd be discussing how to deal with Leo and then run right into him?"

"I agree it's strange. But let's not overthink this. It's quite logical for Leo to think that you'd have children someday now that you're married. And he knows he'll be their biological grandfather."

"Leo treated Jimmy with such kindness and love. Like any child would want from their grandparent. It makes you realize there's a different side to man," I looked at Connor for a reaction.

"Let's keep to our plan and see what happens," Said Connor.

I'm not sure either of us slept soundly that night.

Chapter 10

At the studio, I decided to dive into the background of Eleanor Medill Patterson, whose name was on a key tag, hoping to be distracted from last night's encounter with Leo Barlos. Since Mandy could not locate a living relative, her brief narrative on the accomplished journalist and newspaper owner would have to suffice.

> *Eleanor Patterson, known as Cissy, was born into an accomplished Chicago family. Her grandfather, Joseph Medill, was mayor of Chicago and owner of the Chicago Tribune. The paper later passed to her first cousin Colonel Robert R. McCormick. Joseph Medill Patterson, Cissy's older brother, founded the New York Daily News.*

After a failed marriage to a Polish count, Cissy returned to the U.S. and began her journalism career with William Randolph Hearst at the Washington Herald. Not long after, she became the paper's editor. When Hearst ran into money problems, Cissy bought the newspaper and merged the daily with the afternoon Washington Times to become the Herald-Times.

Learning of Cissy's background was all fine and dandy, but I wanted to know how she met Capone. Fortunately, Mandy included a link to a journal Cissy wrote regarding how she and the head of The Outfit became acquainted.

~

January 1931

My taxi pulled up in front of 93 Palm Island on Miami Beach in January of 1931. Since I was already in town and knew Al Capone, the infamous Chicago kingpin, lived on the Biscayne Bay island, I figured an interview with him would be just the thing to boost newspaper sales. I exited the cab to find a seven-foot-tall concrete wall and a two-story stucco building with a double-wide wooden gate greeting me. I could feel someone's piercing eyes staring at me but didn't see anyone.

"Do you want me to wait?" asked the cabbie. His frown and spiked eyebrows indicated he didn't look too comfortable.

"Just until I get inside," I said.

I tugged the bottom of my dark navy jacket and smoothed the creases in my skirt, then walked up to the gate, head held high. I pulled on the cord of a bell attached to the building; its loud peal signaled my arrival. A little window opened at the top of a door carved into the left gate. A pair of intense eyes peered down at me. The whole experience reminded me of the speakeasies I'd visited in New York.

"Yeah?" asked a gruff voice.

"I'm Cissy Patterson of the 'Herald-Times' in Washington, D.C. If Mr. Capone is available, I'd love to speak with him. Here's my card." I poked my business card through the small window. A large hand clutched it. Knowing that Capone loved the media and being in the limelight, I had an excellent chance to obtain this impromptu interview.

"Wait here," commanded the gruff voice. A few minutes later, he returned. "The boss will see you."

I waved to the cabbie, who drove off in a hurry. Then I slipped through the door and followed gruff voice down the driveway to the front door of the house. I was surprised to see the big man himself—Al Capone—standing at the threshold, waiting for me. We'd never met, but we certainly were aware of who each other was.

"Cissy," said Capone. He held out both hands in greeting. I put my hands in his large, meaty ones, and we exchanged kisses on both cheeks. "Come on in. Let me show you around."

For the next half hour, Capone, nearly six feet tall with the thick neck and broad shoulders of a wrestler, showed me his estate. He'd improved the home by adding mosaic walkways, rock gardens, and fountains, all constructed by the finest artisans available. His pride and joy was the 30- by 60-foot swimming pool, the largest privately-owned pool in Florida. I found his manner kindly, hospitable, and proud.

"You want some lemonade?" he asked.

"Yes, thank you," I said, not wanting to be rude.

Al called for a servant, who rushed to his side. We sat by the pool and talked candidly. Though gruff voice was the only bodyguard I saw, I was convinced a dozen eyes belonging to others followed our every move.

"Why Miami Beach?" I asked. We sat at a small patio table, he on one side, me on the other.

"I got nothing but a raw deal in Chicago, from the law to big business. They never pinned anything on me, and no one in business can say I ever took a dime from them. I don't understand why they can't just leave me alone." Capone gulped his lemonade as though the gesture was a punctuation mark.

(Apparently, he'd forgotten all the people he'd killed or had killed and the legitimate businesses he'd extorted money from for protection.)

"Have you ever considered leaving the U.S. and moving to Italy, like your predecessor John Torrio?"

Capone threw his head back and let out a laugh. Then he stared at me with his ice-cold eyes. "Why should I leave? I've done nothing wrong. You can't find one crime I've been accused of that's stuck. Besides, my wife, kid, and racket are all here. What would I do in Italy?"

"Escape the harassment," I said.

"When you're head of an outfit like I am, you expect a lot of enemies. It comes with the territory. The only way to beat them is at their own game. That's why I have hot shot lawyers both here and Chicago."

"So, what do you think about Prohibition?" I asked. "Do you think the Nineteenth Amendment will ever be repealed?"

"I hope so," he said frankly. "It's the worst thing that's ever happened to the country. Nothing but trouble for all of us. The little guy has become a criminal, and there's no respect for the law."

I was surprised to hear Capone's answer. Besides being one of those who had no respect for the law, his income was substantial before running illegal liquor into the country. With Prohibition, his income had increased exponentially. It had also brought untold pressure on him from local and federal authorities.

"Are you finding Miami as much of a paradise as you expected?" I asked.

"Well, you can't beat the weather," he said, spreading his arms and taking in a deep breath. "But if you're asking me about the people and the law, I'd say it's more like purgatory. No one seems to want me here except the merchants, restaurants, and golf courses that me and my men support. I guess they want my money, but they don't want me."

"I'm sure it takes a while for any community to warm up to someone new. Maybe they just need time," I suggested.

"Perhaps," he said with a hint of sorrow in his voice.

"I have to go, as I have another engagement, but I've certainly enjoyed speaking with you," I said, rising.

"Shall I call you a cab?" Al asked.

"Please."

Once again, Al called his staff, then walked me to the front of the property. We stood there for several minutes chit-chatting before the taxi arrived. When the cab pulled up, Capone unbolted the door in the gate and bid me goodbye.

"Thank you for your time. Good luck," I called back to him as I slipped into the cab.

~

The story of how Cissy and Capone met was interesting, but I couldn't make heads or tails out of why he would include her name on the key tags. Perhaps her being a woman played a role. Or maybe he was impressed because she'd been so bold as to come to his home unannounced and have a pleasant conversation with him. Whatever the reason, he thought enough of her to print her name on a tag.

I finished editing the quilt show and uploaded the segment to our YouTube channel. Next, I printed out a copy of Cissy's story. I'd wander over to Leslie's after dinner later tonight and give it to her.

~

"Have a good day?" Connor greeted me in the kitchen with a hug and kiss.

"Completed the Quilt Show video. So, yes, my day was good. What about you?" I placed my bag on the island counter.

"Got several projects completed, so I'm all caught up. All we need to do now is shop for furniture for the babies' room. How about I take you out for dinner, and we can discuss it?"

I glanced around the kitchen. "I don't smell anything cooking, so I guess that means this is a planned outing. And that means something's up." I crossed my arms over my chest and stared at him. "Care to let me in on the secret you're keeping?"

"I'll tell you over dinner. Where would you like to go tonight?" Connor grabbed my bag from the counter and escorted me, more like pushed me, to the door.

My stomach lurched. "I'm not going to like this, am I?"

"I'm not sure I like it, but it is what it is." Connor held the door for me while I climbed into his truck.

"You're going on another assignment, aren't you? I don't even know why I asked the question. I knew one of these days, the Army would contact you again. I guess they believe you've had enough of a honeymoon."

"I could have said 'no,' but when informed of the situation, I became obligated." Connor drove down Federal Highway into Deerfield Beach.

"More obligated than staying home with your pregnant wife?" I stared out the windshield. I could feel my blood pressure rise.

"Please, Randi, let me explain. Then I'm sure you'll understand why I couldn't refuse.'"

"Somehow, I'm not very hungry."

"Honey, you have to eat. You've got our babies to feed." Connor pulled into the Cove shopping center and stopped at Two Georges.

I hadn't been to the restaurant that sat on the Intracoastal waterway in months. Not since I went there with Seth when Connor was away with the Army. At that moment, I pondered how Seth was doing. We hadn't seen him or Cathy for a while, though he called now and then.

Connor and I walked to the back of the restaurant. An open-air dining area stretched adjacent to a narrow wooden dock next to the water. I was glad I brought a sweater as the night brought a cool sea breeze across the incoming tide, even though the restaurant had lowered three of the heavy plastic sides.

"I wish I could order wine for this conversation," I said, settling in.

"Randi, it's not that bad. Just let me explain. Besides, the doctor said no alcohol until after the babies arrive" Connor ordered us iced tea.

"Okay. I'm all ears," I said, placing my forearms on the table and leaning in.

"Do you remember I told you how I owed your father an obligation for helping me recover from PTSD after

I got discharged, and that's why I was so determined to find his killer?"

"Sure. Dad gave you a job as gardener and pool man and put you up in the cottage." I poured a packet of sweetener and squeezed a lime into my tea.

"Well, this situation is very much like that. In Afghanistan, I had a CO, that's a commanding officer, who stood up for me when things got dicey. Going against convention isn't something you do in the Army without putting your career and reputation on the line. But that's what I and my CO did. I was proved right in the end, but we both could have easily been in deep crap had the situation not worked out in our favor."

The server came to the table and took our order. I waited for him to leave before we continued our conversation.

"Okay, but you're not in the Army anymore, Connor. What obligations do you still have?"

"I realize it's hard for you to understand this, but when you're in the military, there's a bond that forms between you and the men and women you work with and for. That bond doesn't evaporate after discharge. Even though you go your separate ways, there are still deep ties to the country, the military, and the people you served with. This is one of those ties."

"Meaning what, exactly?"

"I can't tell you everything about that old situation due to security issues, but my former CO has asked me for help with a very sensitive situation. It has to do with a charge of sexual harassment."

I was aware of similar stories and even witnessed some at the D.C. TV station. The Me Too movement was based on this scenario—a boss intimidating a staff member, verbally or physically.

"So, he put pressure on a subordinate, and she's pressing charges?"

Connor gulped. I could see he was uncomfortable talking about this.

"Not exactly. The subordinate is pressing charges, but the CO isn't a he; it's a she. And the accuser is male."

I blinked as though I hadn't entirely understood Connor correctly. "What? You're CO was a woman, and you'll be defending her of being accused of sexual harassment by a male subordinate?"

"I'm not a judge advocate, Randi. I won't be defending her. I'll be collecting and looking at the evidence and advising her counsel. I'm not working for the Army. Colonel Patricia Collins has hired me as a private party."

The server brought our dinners—grilled shrimp on skewers, seasoned rice, and steamed broccoli. Connor offered grace.

"And just where are you going, and where will you be staying?" I speared a shrimp and ate it.

"Washington. She works at the Pentagon and made arrangements for me to stay at Fort Belvoir, an Army base." Connor took a bite of his rice, then put down his fork. "Look, honey, I know this is sudden, and you have no frame of reference for this type of relationship except for your father and me, but please understand that I need to do this. Repaying others for times they helped me is paramount to who I am." Connor gazed at me, hoping for understanding.

"I don't have a frame of reference for this, but I do know if one of my friends was in trouble, I'd do whatever I could to help them." I gave Connor a qualified smile of understanding. "When are you leaving?"

"Tomorrow." A sheepish grin spread across Connor's lips.

"Tomorrow! Isn't that a bit sudden?" I was sure the colonel didn't just learn of the accusation.

"It is, but I just got the call today. I should be gone about a week. It's not like I'll be sequestered like last time. I can call you, and you can call me anytime."

"Even every hour?" I asked.

"Even every half hour, if you need to." Connor gave me a wink and one of his mischievous grins.

"What about our meeting with Leo?" I didn't want to wait too long to have this discussion.

"That can keep until I return. None of us is going anywhere."

We finished our dinners with little conversation. I didn't fully understand why Connor had to go, but on the other hand, I understood him well enough to realize he had to do this. He'd never spoken about his time in Afghanistan or the Army, but I knew that he followed through when he committed to something. I was sure this was one of those times.

That night, our lovemaking was as passionate and hungry as the first time on our honeymoon night. In the morning, Connor packed then took an Uber to the West Palm Beach airport so I wouldn't have to drive him. I'd go on with my life at the studio and with the investigation as I had several times before when he was on assignment with the Army. I'd miss him like crazy, but my nature wouldn't let me feel helpless while he was away.

Chapter 11

I missed taking the information about Cissy Patterson over to Leslie's last night for obvious reasons, so I visited her in the morning and took over the report. We sipped tea while she read the journal.

"Her story still leaves me wondering why Capone included her name on a tag. But you know what they say about some women—they have a special kind of sympathy for gangsters. Maybe Cissy was one of them. Maybe that's why she visited him in the first place and wrote about her visit. She did say some flattering things about him."

"Perhaps, but being a media person, it's more likely she was looking for a good story. Something that would boost newspaper sales. She was a very competitive person."

"I guess we'll never know either way," said Leslie with a sigh.

"Anything yet from David about his investigation into the banks?" I leaned forward, hoping to hear something encouraging.

"Actually, he did phone last night and wants to get together with you and Connor tomorrow so he could give us the news while we're together. Are you two available?"

I sat back, a pout on my face. "Unfortunately, not. Connor left this morning for D.C. He has an assignment with his former commanding officer and will probably be gone about a week."

"By the look on your face, I see you aren't too happy about that."

"I was hoping all these assignments would be over after we married, but I can't stop him from doing what he was trained for and loves. It would be like telling me to give up the studio. I'd be miserable. I wouldn't wish that on him." I got up, refilled my mug with hot water, and dunked my still good tea bag.

"Then, how about you and I meet with David? You can always take notes and tell Connor about the conversation later. That way, we can keep moving on with the investigation." Leslie looked at me expectantly.

"I've lost my cook for a while, so having dinner out sounds like a plan."

Since I was pretty much caught up in the studio and wouldn't be taping Archie's show until next week, I decided to go shopping for furniture for the babies' room after I left Leslie's. I knew Connor had mentioned doing this, but he wasn't here, and I didn't think he'd be upset with my getting an early start on the task. Shopping for baby furniture would take my mind off his absence and make me feel we were still connected even at a distance.

That's when I remembered the card Mrs. Jamison gave me. I headed up Federal Highway and pulled into the

Jamison Furniture parking lot. I hadn't been in the upscale store for over a decade. While the store didn't specialize in baby furniture, it did have a section of choice baby beds and dressers with changing pads.

"May I help you? I'm Christina and would be happy to show you our furniture. Selecting for yourself or someone else?" Christina held a clipboard and gave me a generous ruby smile.

"I'm selecting for myself. Twins."

"Congratulations," she said. "Your first?"

"My first everything," I said. The words brought a wave of anxiety rushing through me.

"Then let me show you our newest design. It enables the crib to grow with the child by converting from newborn to toddler and beyond. It's intended to last many years."

"Sounds like a great idea. A woman must have designed the crib," I said with a chuckle.

Christina gave me a tour of the furniture and showed me how the bed converts from an infant to a toddler bed using rails.

"Oh, here. Let me give you this. Mrs. Jamison said to present it to the associate who helped me." I pulled out the card Mrs. Jamison gave me at the studio.

"You must be Mrs. Romero, owner of A Stitch in Time." She wrote my name on the back of the card and stuck it under the clip on her board.

I pulled back. "How did you know?"

"Mrs. Jamison told all of us to be on the lookout for you. She said you were most accommodating, and she was thrilled to have her quilt purchased by the planetarium."

"The quilt was lovely. I'm glad we could help Mrs. Jamison show off her handiwork to so many others."

"So, did you like this set of furniture?"

"I do like the white set, but I'd have to bring my husband by for final approval. Right now, he's out of town." Whether the twins were boys or girls or one each, the white furniture would fit in with whatever décor we chose.

"Of course. Let me just note that on our form, and you can give me a call when your husband returns. Do you have a business card? I'll attach it to the form."

I handed Christina my card.

"You know, Mrs. Jamison's card allows you to a substantial discount. She gives out very few."

"I didn't know," I said, surprised by the revelation.

"Well, give me a call when your husband returns, and Jamison's will do what we can to make being new parents a special time."

As I left the store, I couldn't help but remember what Connor said to me when we first met Mrs. Jamison—"Doing favors for people who don't deserve it can turn out to be a blessing."

He was right.

I hadn't connected with my best friend, Rachel, who was also the studio's COO and marketing genius, for our girls' night out yet, so now would be a good time with Connor out of town. I drove back to the studio to see if she was in.

"Wow. You're actually in your office," I said, taking a seat across from her. With her myriad duties, she rarely occupied her office. Most of the time, she was out making calls.

"Yep. Catching up on paperwork. What's up? You feeling okay?"

"Doing fine," I said, rubbing my hands over my tummy, though I never knew when nausea would return. "Connor left on an assignment this morning, and that means I'm free for a girls' night out. When's a good time for you?"

Rachel looked at her phone and brought up her calendar. "No can do until next week. How about Tuesday?"

"Great. I've got you down. Do you mind if we meet at Boca Grande? I'll order something in. We never got around to discussing my old bedroom's redo with the wedding and all. I still want to do that, so maybe we could talk about that, too."

"Sounds good. What else is going on? I'm dying to hear about your new investigation. Didn't you say the case was Capone's keys? Sounds intriguing."

"I'll tell you all about the investigation when I see you on Tuesday. I've got to check in with accounting, so I'll leave you to your work." I blew Rachel a kiss.

On my way over to accounting, I ran into Archie.

"All set for the taping next week?" I asked.

"Randall and I have been practicing. I think this will be a good show."

"They're all good shows. That reminds me, Create TV phoned again. They're still looking for us to join their lineup. Have you given the opportunity any more consideration?"

"Miss Randi, I think it's still too early for us. We've only done a few shows, and although we've developed quite a following, I'd like to have a few more tapings under my belt before we jump into national TV. I hope you understand." Archie gave me puppy dog eyes.

"Only when you're ready," I said.

~

"So, this is where you went on your first date?" I gazed across the table at Leslie and David as we sat in a booth at Max's Grille in Mizner Park.

"It was a special night," said David, eyeing Leslie caringly.

"Well, I'm dying to try their oriental dish." I perused the menu while our server took our drink orders—iced tea all around.

"I understand Connor's away on an assignment. I'm sorry he couldn't join us," said David.

"Me, too. He's in Washington working with his former commanding officer on a case of harassment. She's the one accused."

"Would that be Colonel Pat Collins?" asked David.

"How did you know that?" I couldn't imagine how he knew who she was. But on second thought, he did retire from the Pentagon. Even though he was in the Air Force and she was in the Army, I was sure everyone was aware of each other's business.

"Word travels fast in Washington, and I still know a lot of people there who love to share the local gossip. You, of all people, should have experienced that, being in the media."

Shock, like a lightning bolt, surged through me. "Oh my gosh! What if one of the stations covers the story of her case and interviews Connor?"

"I'm sure he can handle a few questions," said Leslie.

"You don't know the media. They'll make something of nothing, and they may even uncover the incident in Afghanistan that endeared Connor to the Colonel. He didn't tell me what happened for security reasons, but there's always someone who will talk while looking for their fifteen minutes of fame." My eyes searched David and Leslie's for comfort.

"I didn't know Colonel Collins personally. She came to the Pentagon way after me, but her reputation is impeccable. I doubt they'll be able to prove the harassment claim is legit. A male subordinate claiming to be harassed by their female commanding officer? That certainly is a switch on the typical harassment case."

"My point exactly," I said. "It's a Me Too in reverse and right up the alley of the investigative reporters. They'll turn over every stone to find someone to misrepresent the facts. I've got to warn Connor."

"After dinner, I hope. I don't think much will happen in the next hour. It's nighttime," said David.

I wanted to hear what David found out about the banks in our Capone mystery but was so upset about the possibilities of Connor being stalked by the media, all I could do was push my oriental chicken and rice around my plate. We set another time to get together to talk about the banks.

~

"Hey, babe, how's everything going?" I asked when Connor called that night.

"It's quite the case. Wish I could tell you about it, but I'll have to wait until I get back, when it's over. "

"Well, I wanted to give you a heads up regarding your case. Since the uniqueness of the situation has become so high-profile, one of the networks might get in touch to interview you. They're always looking for sensational topics and have ways to ferret out all kinds of people associated with them. I wouldn't be surprised if you hear from someone."

"You mean like your old coworker, Kevin Marks?"

I inhaled sharply. "That little rat?"

"Uh-huh."

"He doesn't even work Pentagon news. He works Capitol Hill news." I couldn't imagine why he would contact Connor.

"That may be, but he mentioned your name and knew we were married. Maybe he believed he could get the inside scoop if he threw your name around."

"You didn't fall for that ploy, did you?"

"Honey, I'm an investigator, a trained interrogator, and I know how to keep secrets. Don't worry about me. He's the one who should be worried."

"Okay. Just be cautious. Kevin's not to be trusted." I had first-hand experience with his divisive tactics when he stabbed me in the back on a story I did before leaving the station. Though the incident wasn't the reason I resigned, it was the catalyst that made me take a good hard look at my profession and decide I needed to move on.

"Got everything under control," Connor said with confidence. "Oh, I meant to tell you. On the key tags, Curtis texted me to say he's still working on them. There's a new technique called Video Spectral Comparator 2000 that allows him to identify obscure handwriting and determine the quality or origin of the paper. The only trouble is, it's quite costly. Let's see what he turns up using conventional techniques first, then we can decide whether to go farther."

"Sounds good. I look forward to getting Curtis's report."

Connor and I talked for a few more minutes, then hung up. After our conversation, I was far more at ease and tucked myself into bed with my feline companion beside me. Bigfoot and I hadn't had the bed all to ourselves since the wedding. In a way, I enjoyed it.

Chapter 12

I sat in my office at the studio, checking off my to-do list to ensure everything was ready for Archie and Randall's headboard upholstering taping. They had already moved their equipment and props into the studio and rehearsed. Today's taping was the first time they were taking an upholstery project from simple to wow. I couldn't wait to see the finished project.

As usual, I had contracted several gifted students from the local high school communications magnet program to do the taping along with me. They were already in the studio testing their audio and visual equipment. I joined them after I called Leslie and set another meeting with David. This time, he'd come to the house.

"Okay. Everyone ready?" I had informed the fabric and upholstery staff of the taping, locked the studio doors, and hung the "Taping In Progress" signs on the outside. For several hours, we wouldn't be disturbed.

"Hi, upholstery newbies. This is Archie…"

"And Randall..."

"...of A Stitch in Time here in Boca Raton, Florida. We typically take you on an exciting adventure to discover and recover what's behind your behind. But today, we're going to move a bit higher and show you how to upholster a headboard. But not only that, we're going to show you how to take it from ordinary to wow! Are you ready?" Archie looked directly into the camera and wiggled his eyebrows as he usually did when introducing the show.

Between their bantering, jokes, and explanations, Archie and Randall took a large piece of plywood cut to the shape and dimensions of a queen-sized headboard. They covered it with padding and an attractive dark neutral print material. Their efforts made a comfortable and beautiful headboard, but the transformation was just beginning.

Next, they added upholstery tacks on the perimeter, then cording that crisscrossed the headboard. Finally, they embellished the headboard with accent buttons in the middle of the crisscrosses to create a tufted look. By the time they finished the lesson, the headboard had become more than a plain fabric-covered piece of plywood. It became an elegant piece of furniture that would be the centerpiece of any bedroom.

"And remember," said Archie, closing with a smile. "Keep God in front, and you won't have to worry about your behind."

"That's a wrap. Good job, everyone." I gave Archie, Randall, and the taping crew high fives. "Are you going to put the headboard up for sale as you've done with the other pieces from the shows?"

"Sure thing," said Randall. "The customers love what we do and appreciate being able to take home the real thing."

"It doesn't hurt business, either," said Archie with a laugh. "I'll bet we get at least ten orders for custom headboards after this. Better stock up on material." He gave me a wide smile.

"I'll make sure to give Adele a heads up."

Just at that moment, the studio door unlocked, and Adele rushed in, her brows pinched together. She pulled me aside.

"It's all over the news," she said, out of breath.

"Whatever are you talking about?" I eyed her curiously.

"Connor and that lady colonel in Washington. They're having an affair."

"What?" I asked, my heart thumping.

"John just called me from the police station. He said he saw the story on the news. Someone took a photo of Connor at dinner with the colonel. She was giving him a sexy look while whispering in his ear. The image made it look like more than a professional relationship. You may want to speak with Connor."

My hands shook as I pulled out my phone and turned it on. My cell indicated Connor had phoned me repeatedly.

"Excuse me," I said to Adele.

I rushed to my office, my heart in my throat. I pulled up the news article and photo in question when I got behind the closed door. The sight of it was like a gut punch.

When Connor told me she was a colonel, I envisioned an older woman with short-cropped hair and a seasoned look. This woman was nowhere near that. Patricia looked maybe in her late forties with a heart-shaped, attractive face, long brown hair that cascaded over her shoulders, and green eyes. I swallowed hard. Adele was right; it did look like they were involved. Tears pricked my eyes.

Just then, my phone rang—Connor.

"I've been trying to reach you for hours," he said, his voice tense, irritated.

"My phone is always off when I'm taping in the studio. Adele just told me John Kester called. Something about you and the colonel having an affair." Heat coursed up my neck.

"Typical Washington politics," Connor huffed. "If they can discredit Patricia, it'll look bad for the defense. They'll think she wanted the affair with her Lieutenant subordinate, and she was the aggressor, not him."

"Well, I've seen the photo, Connor. You did go to dinner with her, and she did whisper in your ear." I held my breath. "Just how much portrayed in the photo is true?"

"We went out to dinner to discuss the case with her Judge Advocate, but he had gone to the bar at the particular moment someone took the photo. The noise level in the restaurant was so high we could hardly hear each other, so she leaned in."

"Well, the photo does look suggestive, Connor, and Patricia is a striking woman. If I didn't know you better, I could see how someone could easily misinterpret the situation." My heart pounded in my throat as I paced the room, my neck getting hotter with each step.

"I suppose, but rest assured, we're not having an affair. Our relationship is purely professional, not what the media is trying to portray."

I let out a deep sigh. Having been in Washington for so many years and knowing how it worked, I needed to give Connor the benefit of the doubt.

"Well, I warned you. Now you're just another cog in the wheel of D.C. sensationalism."

"Don't worry, Randi. I can play their game if I have to."

"Connor, I love you because you don't play their game. Please don't turn into one of them."

I was all too aware of what *they* looked like and how *they* played. I'd been one of them for a long time, overlooking the truth to keep my bosses and the Washington power brokers happy. I was so glad I'd returned to Boca, hundreds of miles away from Washington and its thirst for scandals. Not that small towns didn't have their share, but the scale in Washington was many times what it might be elsewhere.

"Since what's reported here isn't often the truth, keep your phone on so I can reach you if something like this happens again. I hate you had to hear about this second hand. I'll call you tonight as always. Just know that I love you," said Connor.

I was saddened to think he had fallen into D.C.'s grip as we ended our call.

"Everything alright?" asked Adele when I re-entered the studio.

"It will be," I said.

Adele hugged me, then returned to the store. The students were packing up the audio and visual equipment and storing it in the control room. After they left, I sat, trying to regain my composure. Had the news of the incident in D.C. unnerved me? Yes. But I couldn't let it unravel me. I trusted Connor, and while he was in Washington, I needed to focus on my job in the studio and the Capone case.

~

I had David and Leslie over for dessert several days later to discuss his findings on the banks. We sat in the sunroom. I served tea and blueberry cobbler, a simple recipe I picked up on the internet. Everyone received an ample and yummy helping.

"I'm so sorry about the last time we got together. After our discussion, my mind just couldn't focus on the banks. I do apologize," I said to Leslie and David.

"No harm done," said David. "It's not as though this is something that has to be solved immediately. Sure, it's interesting, but whatever was in the safe deposit boxes can wait."

"Thanks. So, let's see what you found," I said.

David pulled out a red folder and opened it. Inside were several printed pages. He scanned the first one, then launched into his findings.

"I started with Illinois because that seemed the most reasonable place to look since Capone spent time in Chicago before coming to Florida, and we're not sure when he started putting the money into the lockbox."

"Sounds logical." Leslie gave David a reassuring nod.

"So, this is how Illinois distributes unclaimed items in safe deposit boxes. If the rent goes unpaid or the lease expires for five years, the Illinois Department of Revenue takes possession of the unclaimed contents of boxes. They keep the items for three more years then hold an auction. They hold any money until claimed. Kind of like Florida, except Florida, holds all items indefinitely."

"So, by this time, if it were an item, it would have been auctioned. But the money would still be there?" asked Leslie.

"Correct," said David. "Every state has its own rules on how they handle the unclaimed contents of safe deposit boxes. But here's something I found quite interesting. During the Depression, 1929 to the late 1930s, hundreds of banks failed. The federal government kept the contents of their unclaimed safe deposit boxes. In Florida, this happened even earlier because Florida's banking industry started going bust by the mid-1920s. So, the contents of Florida safe deposit boxes could have been sent there that early."

"Yeah, but Capone didn't come into power until 1925, and he didn't know he was going to jail until 1930. By that time, he was in Florida," I said.

"Right. So I checked the names you gave me from the key tags with the Illinois unclaimed property, and none of the names matched. I could only surmise that Capone took out the boxes closer to his going to jail, and he took them out in Florida banks. That's a good thing because if something is left—money or items—Florida would still have them."

"Did you check the names in Florida?" I asked.

"I did," David said, his eyes sparkling and his smile broad. "Of the four names you gave me, all of them matched on the Florida website. So we know that Capone put something in the boxes, probably money, in those individuals' names."

"Yes!" I said with a fist pump.

"And now, their heirs can claim the money." Leslie's clapped softly.

"Well, it's not going to be that simple. It's incumbent upon the individual to check with the state to see if there is anything in their or a relative's name. Most of these people don't even know to check. So, now that we know something is there and we have names, is it our responsibility to contact the relatives to let them know?" asked David. He transferred his gaze from me to Leslie.

"How would we do that? There could be dozens of relatives to any one of the names." Leslie's tone expressed exasperation.

"My point exactly," said David. "Even though it would be interesting to know what's in the boxes, in the long run, we may never know. We'd need to leave the descendants to duke it out for possession, and that could take years."

"Unless we could find a single descendant. That would be the piece de resistance," I said, eyes wide with hope.

"Even then, there are a lot of hoops to jump through for the individual to prove they are the rightful heir of the deceased—death certificates, wills, social security numbers, affidavits, and more. The descendant would need to go through a great deal of verification before the state turned over any of the contents." David gathered his papers and placed them back into the file.

"First, we need to establish whether the box actually belonged to Capone and who the other names are so Mandy can see if there are any single descendants," I said.

"Yes. But if the box belonged to Capone, the people whose names are on the tags won't own the contents anyway. Whatever was inside would belong to the U.S. government, as Connor pointed out earlier. That's because Capone may have obtained the items through ill-gotten gains. The government would have to prove that, of course, but I'm sure that wouldn't be too hard." David tossed the file onto the coffee table.

"So, until Connor's buddy, Curtis, can supply us with some additional information, we're no further than we were," said Leslie, her smile turning into a frown.

"True," I said. "But we have to keep looking for the people and see what their connection to Capone was. Already, we have four people connected to him. That doesn't prove Capone owned the box, as it's only circumstantial. But my money says it points in his direction."

"I agree. Let's wait and see what Curtis comes up with, and then we can continue our investigation. It's been fun so far. And you never know where an investigation like this will take us. Besides, there's another mystery here we've forgotten. What do any of these people or the contents of the safe deposit boxes have to do with Derick Eastway's death?" David shrugged and spread his hands.

"That's right," said Leslie, sitting forward. "Well, I'm for moving forward."

"Great. Then on with the show…I mean investigation!" I punched my index finger into the air for emphasis.

~

When Connor called that night, I told him about meeting with Leslie and David and the outcome of David's research. He encouraged us to press on with the following surprise.

"Good news, my love. Curtis contacted me; he has some results. I've emailed them to you."

"This calls for a happy dance." I got up and gyrated around the bedroom. Good thing only Bigfoot was watching. My dancing wasn't pretty. "How are things on your end?"

"The same. The case should wrap up by Friday, and I should be home Saturday."

"No more issues?" I asked.

"None so far, but we've still got a few days left, so anything can happen." His voice sounded tired.

"Well, I'm sure your CO is glad to have you on her side. Are you getting enough sleep?"

Connor laughed. "That's one thing in short supply. Don't be upset if it takes me a few days to catch up when I get home."

"You can sleep all you want. I'll just be happy to have you home. Just remember, you'll need to save some bedtime for me."

"That goes without saying. Gotta hit the sack, honey. I'll speak to you tomorrow. Keep a lookout for my email."

As soon as we hung up, I accessed my email and printed out the results of Curtis's research. He made out five names on the six key tags, all men. Tomorrow, I'd check them against the names of those I found in the books to see what relationship the men had to Capone.

Before going to sleep, I emailed the list to David to check against the Florida unclaimed property division and sent a copy to Mandy to see if she could locate any relatives. I also printed out one list for Leslie. That left eight illegible key tags. Although Curtis had made out some impressions with his sophisticated equipment, time and salt had destroyed the rest of them, rendering the tags unreadable. Only one tag remained unaccounted for—number nine. If only I could find it.

Chapter 13

After spending some time editing the upholstery video, I turned my attention to finding out who the five men were whose names Curtis could identify on the key tags. I recognized two right off the bat—Jack McGurn and Eliot Ness. Jack McGurn was a member of the Chicago Outfit and one of Capone's hitmen, bodyguards, and chief enforcers. Eliot Ness was a Treasury Agent credited with finally ending Capone's career as head of The Outfit, though not directly. I looked up the history of McGurn and Ness. There were copious amounts of information online about them.

In short, John "Machine Gun" McGurn was one of Capone's trusted insiders. He was a flashy dresser, a top-notch golfer, and said to be the primary planner of the St. Valentine's Day Massacre in 1929, where seven of the rival Bugs Moran gang members were assassinated. Though charged in the case, McGurn never went to trial due to the alibi provided by Louise Rolfe, his girlfriend, who later became his wife. She claimed the two spent the day together. Eventually, McGurn lost his life in what many believe was a revenge killing. He was only thirty-four at the time.

I figured Capone put McGurn's name on a tag because of his loyalty to The Outfit, but Ness's name stumped me. The only logical explanation for his name on a tag was that it was easy to remember—no apology here like Ilsa Carpuci or Lena Galluccio. Ness was on the tag because he was someone Capone wouldn't easily forget. Perhaps someone on a vendetta list he'd have The Outfit take out once he was out of prison.

With President Hoover's hardy approval, a handful of Prohibition agents were assigned to reign in Capone's illegal breweries and supply routes and gather evidence of his violation of the National Prohibition Act. Eliot Ness, at age twenty-seven, was chosen to lead the squad. Scheduled raids began in March 1931, just five months before Capone when to prison. The first six months of the campaign proved highly successful, closing down hundreds of breweries and costing Capone millions in potential revenues. Though Capone's men tried to bribe and intimidate the agents, the term "untouchables" became their nickname due to their unwavering commitment to justice and resistance to corruption.

Though a treasury agent was the one who discovered the accounting ledger that finally brought Capone to justice, Ness was among the federal agents who escorted the gangster to the Dearborn Station to board the train to the Atlanta Federal Penitentiary after his conviction. There, Capone would serve a one-year sentence before being transferred to Alcatraz in California. This encounter was the only time Capone and Ness were known to have met in person. Mandy would continue to look for McGurn's and Ness's heirs, but I was more interested in learning about the three men whose names I didn't recognize—Bob Hanley, John Orr Sr., and Dr. Homer Pearson. I needed to check the books I'd ordered on Capone to see if the authors mentioned any of these three men. And, of course, Mandy would try to find their heirs as well.

I typed up my notes on McGurn and Ness and printed them out for Leslie. She'd want to know their backgrounds. As soon as I got any info on the other three men from Mandy and David, Leslie and I would contact their relatives. I hoped we'd have as much success with them as we'd had with the others.

~

The rest of the week was quiet, too quiet. I missed Connor, so did Bigfoot. I swam laps in the pool every night and read the Capone books, but that wasn't enough to keep my mind from wondering what was transpiring in D.C. Even with Connor's nightly phone calls and reassurances that things were going well, I was lonely without his arms around me and his goodnight kisses. While only a day before he'd be back, I could hardly wait.

That night as I undressed, I could see my belly enlarging—transformed from the flat and toned abdomen into one starting to protrude. Thankfully, I wore PJs with elastic waistbands to accommodate my expanding waistline, but it wouldn't be long until I had to buy new clothes. The change made me excited and apprehensive at the same time. I guess most women pregnant for the first time reacted that way.

~

Connor rushed through the door around noon on Saturday. Dropping his bags to the floor, he found me in the kitchen. He wrapped his arms around me and planted a hot kiss on my mouth.

"I guess this means the Colonel was acquitted," I said when he let me go. "You could have told me over the phone."

"Wouldn't have quite the same impact," he said with a wink.

"True," I said, gazing into his eyes.

"And how are the twins?" Connor stood back, eyeing my tummy.

"Growing," I said. "I placed his hand on my belly so he could feel my beginning bulge.

"Can't wait to see the pumpkin. You'll be beautiful." Taking my face in his hands, he kissed me again.

"Enough of that, Mr. Romero. I'm dying to hear about the trial. I could only find snippets on the news. I guessed when the media realized you weren't having an affair with the Colonel, they dropped their interest. I want the inside scoop."

"I did a bang-up job, if I do say so myself." Connor grabbed a grape from the fruit bowl and tossed it into his mouth.

"So, you were the star of the show?"

"Something like that." He leaned against the island, a smug look on his face. "It was my sharp interrogation techniques that broke the case."

"Well, I'm certain the Colonel was most grateful for your help."

"She was. It was nice to be involved in such an important cause. And the fact that I could support Patricia when she needed it like she did for me was most rewarding."

"So what's next for you now that you've finished the cottage and baby's room? Except for the furniture, that is."

"I've been asked to take on a couple of other assignments but wanted to talk with you first."

"Can that discussion wait until tomorrow? I'd like us just to enjoy each other tonight."

"Then come on, Mrs. Romero. Let's go enjoy each other." Connor took my hand and led me upstairs.

~

"So, how's the Capone case coming?" asked Connor after church on Sunday. He flipped hamburgers on the grill while I dried off in a lounge chair by the pool after my laps.

"Good. Thanks to your friend Curtis, we're honing in on the last of the keys we can read. I'm waiting to hear back from Mandy and David. Then Leslie and I will be able to finish our work with the relatives."

"Good news. And key number nine? Ever find that one?"

"Nope. I looked again in the kitchen and can't imagine what had happened to it. Oh, I meant to tell you, while you were gone, I went up to Jamison's Furniture and tentatively picked out a suite of baby furniture. I'd like you to take a look at it. If you approve, we can put in an order. Also, I presented the card Mrs. Jamison gave me to the salesperson. She told me the card represents a substantial discount. All because you treated Mrs. Jamison and her quilt with such dignity."

"Huh," said Connor, tilting his head to the side. "One never knows when a good deed will go rewarded."

"Now that you're back, we do have a couple of lingering issues to discuss, including Leo Barlos and future assignments."

"How about we discuss them over our burgers? They're almost ready."

Our conversation over baked beans, potato salad, and burgers proved lively, especially regarding Connor's future assignments. In the end, we decided he wouldn't accept projects that required more than two weeks away at any one time, and he would stop accepting them two months before the babies' due date. We would make an appointment with Leo as soon as possible to inform him of my pregnancy and discuss his future non-relationship with the children and us.

Chapter 14

Connor loved the furniture I tentatively picked out for the babies' room, so we put in an order. When we put down a deposit, there appeared to be some mistake. The discount Mrs. Jamison's card gave us cut the cost of the furniture in half. Connor giving Mrs. Jamison a second chance with her quilt was a lesson I wouldn't easily forget.

While editing Archie's headboard video at the studio, I received a call from Mandy.

"You must lead a charmed life, Randi. All the stars seem to be aligning in your direction."

I smiled. "I take it that means you've had success finding some of the heirs?"

"Success with every one of them, and all the heirs live in Florida. I've emailed the information along with a final invoice since I'm assuming you won't need my services on this case anymore."

"You've been wonderful and so accommodating, Mandy. I'm sure we'll use you again. I'll get payment out to you immediately."

"More than receiving that, I'd love to know how your investigation turns out."

I laughed. "We'd all like to know that about now, but no problem. I'll let you know. It certainly has been an intriguing case."

"Oh, I meant to tell you. I did find that of the people I searched, only one has a single living relative. I think you were especially interested in that, weren't you?"

Yes!" I said enthusiastically. "They might be the key to the whole case."

"Well, good luck. I can't wait to hear the outcome."

I accessed my email and printed out the information on Pearson, Orr, and Hanley. I'd read my copy this afternoon and give a copy to Leslie when I got home.

I scanned Mandy's report, excited about what she'd found. Leslie would find the information just as interesting, and I could hardly wait to show her tonight.

"Hey, girlfriend, are we still on for tomorrow night?"

I looked up to find Rachel standing in the doorway of the control room.

"Got it on my calendar," I said, rising and giving her a hug. "My place at 7 p.m. We'll eat, take a look at the bedroom, and I'll show you the furniture we've picked out for the babies' room."

"And you'll tell me all about Capone's keys. Right?"

"Of course."

"Oh, I meant to tell you. I got a call from a boy named Jimmy Markam. He said he met you on the Deerfield Beach pier, and you told him to contact me. What's that all about?"

"He's ten and wants to get involved with the studio and the dogs."

"Are you sure that's all there is to it? He said you knew his grandfather."

"I do, but it's a bit complicated. How about we table that conversation until tomorrow? Then I'll tell you everything." I bit my lip; moisture formed in my eyes.

Rachel grasped my hand. "You okay?"

"Sure," I said.

"I'll see you tomorrow night," said Rachel, squeezing my hand before leaving.

~

Leslie and I sat at her dinette with cups of tea and a plate of shortbread cookies. We went over the reports Mandy sent.

"Look here," said Leslie. "Mandy's report says John Orr used to be Capone's neighbor on Palm Island. He lived two lots down. I'd love to know his story."

"I guess we can ask his granddaughter since she lives in the Panhandle."

"The next guy on our list is Bob Hanley. He was a pilot, and his son was a pilot. What did flying have to do with Capone?" I knew boats transported the contraband liquor to shore, and then trucks and cars took the cases to their final destination, but I hadn't heard of the rumrunners using planes.

"Pilots used to fly the booze into Florida from the Bahamas using sea and land planes. I remember hearing stories of how some of the pilots landed on the fairways of Florida golf courses to unload their cargo. I'm sure the golfers were surprised. And look at this, Bob Hanley's son lives in Hollywood, Florida, so we've got another contact close by. Isn't that wonderful?" Leslie clapped softly like she always did when excited.

"The third man, Homer Pearson, was a physician living in Miami during the 1920s. He has a son living in Lady Lake in central Florida. He's a pastor and Homer's last living relative. He's the one we need to concentrate on if we want to know what might be in the safe deposit box," I said with confidence. The information Mandy provided seemed to get better and better.

"The son's got to be in his eighties or nineties by now. I guess we'd better contact him as soon as possible. You never know what might happen to someone his age."

I drew back and shook my head. "Aren't you in your eighties, too, Miss Historian?"

Leslie leaned in and spoke in a whisper as though she was about to impart some grand secret. "Yeah, but I never think of myself as being that age. I'm young at heart." She punctuated the statement with a warm smile.

I laughed. "That you are, my friend. That you are."

"How about I call Mr. Orr's granddaughter, and you call Pastor Pearson? I'll also contact Mr. Hanley and make an appointment to see him. We'll have ourselves a little road trip down to Hollywood, maybe even lunch on the boardwalk at the beach. I haven't been down there in years." Leslie's eyes twinkled at the possibility.

"Great. I'll talk to you tomorrow." I rose, hugged Leslie, and wandered back through the secret gate to the house. Bigfoot padded alongside me, letting himself in through the kitty door in the utility room.

"Have a nice visit?" asked Connor. He sat in the sunroom watching TV. I eased myself beside him.

"Seeing Leslie always makes for a pleasant visit. Oh, I forgot to tell you, Rachel's coming for dinner tomorrow night. It's a girls' night out, and I'm ordering in sushi. I want her to take a look at my old room for a makeover. She was supposed to work on the bedroom right after redoing ours, but somehow that got postponed. Do you suppose it had something to do with an impromptu wedding?" I gave Connor a peck on the cheek.

"With months before the babies arrive, it seems like good timing. After the twins get here, the place will be in chaos with my parents in the cottage and taking care of two squalling infants. Just keep in mind that room will eventually become one of the bedrooms when the kids get older. Let's not make it too formal."

"Of course. Leave it to Rachel. She'll make it beautiful without the formality. Do you want me to order sushi for you?"

"No. I think I'll call Seth and Cathy and run up to West Palm Beach to see them. I haven't seen my sister in a long time, though we've texted."

"Good idea. Tell both 'hi' for me. Why don't you invite them down for a cookout soon? It would be nice to catch up. And we could invite Adele and Kester, too. "

"And Leslie, Archie, and Karen? A reunion of sorts?"

"Yeah. Wouldn't that be fun? You can show them the work you've done in the cottage and babies' room. They'll be so impressed."

"Okay, okay," said Connor, holding up his hands in surrender and giving me a wide grin. "You've talked me into it. I'll start making a menu. See how long it will take Rachel to finish up your and the babies' rooms, and we can include them in the tour as well. And we'll add her and Todd to the guest list. "

"You're the best," I said, kissing him tenderly.

~

Rachel arrived at seven. We ate at the island in the kitchen and spread out images on the counter of our ideas for my old bedroom transformation. By the time we finished eating, we had a design plan. It wasn't a large job, and Rachel estimated completion within a month. We then turned our conversation to the studio and nonprofit. We agreed to hold two more fundraisers over the next nine months. As Rachel gathered the design images from the counter, I prepared dessert and coffee.

"I'm dying to hear about Capone's keys. Tell me everything, and don't leave anything out," Rachel warned. She carried plates of chocolate cream cake into the sunroom while I followed with the mugs of coffee.

"It started with a visit to the house by a woman I didn't know." I proceeded to tell her the entire story up to now. "And so, we have three more men to speak with. Hopefully, the preacher, who is the last of the Dr.'s relatives, will be able to open one of the safe deposit boxes. Then we'll finally discover what's inside." I sipped my coffee in between bites of cake.

"Oh my gosh. Your investigation reminds me of something that happened the year you and I were born. My parents used to laugh about this show as one of TV's most anticipated events. Ever heard of Geraldo Rivera?"

"Who hasn't in the TV business? He's worn a host of hats in his career—investigative reporter, talk show host, war correspondent, and many others. Controversy seems to follow him like a shadow."

"Then you know of the 1986 TV special when he opened Capone's vault in the abandoned Lexington Hotel in Chicago where Capone's gang used to headquarter?" Rachel sat forward. A wide grin spread across her face, and her eyes sparkled as though she would burst if she didn't tell me some secret.

"Sure. My parents used to talk about it, too. Locksmiths opened the vault only to find nothing inside.

So?" What did this story have to do with the safe deposit boxes?

"Do you realize you're sitting on the most fabulous fundraising event ever? Forget the events we just talked about. This is it, Randi!" Rachel jumped up and hurriedly paced about the room.

"What are you talking about, Rachel?" My brow furrowed as I shot her a questioning look.

She plopped beside me on the couch and took my hands.

"The safe deposit box. We have it or a facsimile opened in the studio with the key that's been in hiding in the lockbox for almost one hundred years. Capone's lockbox. Picture this..." Rachel adjusted herself on the couch and gestured with her hands. "The studio is packed with a live audience who pays top dollar to be there in person. In addition, millions are viewing online as we live stream the event for which they purchased tickets. Of course, I'm just thinking off the top of my head. I'm sure this event would need much more discussion, but we've got our moneymaker staring us right in the face. What do you think?"

I let her concept sink in. "It sounds good, but I don't think we're far enough along to know if we've even got a box to open."

"You're missing the point, Randi. Like the opening of the Lexington vault in Chicago, it doesn't matter if there's something or nothing inside the safe deposit box. It's the intrigue created that there might be that's important. There was nothing in the vault at the Lexington Hotel but dust, yet the anticipation built around the possibility was enormous. Over thirty million viewers watched the show. Can you imagine what kind of impact even a fraction of those viewers could have on the studio, shop, store, and nonprofit? How many dogs could be adopted?"

"It does sound exciting, but I need to think about it. We don't even know if the lockbox actually belonged to Capone. And, I'd like to get Connor's opinion. I see the potential; I do. I'm just not sure I want to turn our investigations into a sideshow."

"Not a sideshow, Randi, an opportunity. People will want to know what Capone put into the boxes and who the people were whose names were on the key tags. The story of Thelma touching Capone's face is priceless. And the other stories, too. The story of the lockbox is a once-in-a-lifetime chance to spread the word about the business and the dogs. Isn't that why you built the studio in the first place?" Rachel gazed at me with wide eyes.

"It is," I confessed. "I guess I just didn't want it to grow so fast, beyond my ability to control it. And with the twins coming. It just might be too fast for us right now."

"Okay," said Rachel, reaching for my hands. "Let's both take a deep breath. Sleep on it. We can talk again tomorrow or the day after, once we've had an opportunity to give it some more consideration. What do you say?"

I hesitated, trying to make sense of everything.

"Yes. Okay." I smiled at Rachel, and we hugged each other. "We'll take some time to digest this conversation and the possibilities."

"Good. Now, how about telling me about the young boy on the pier?"

I laughed. "I think we've had enough excitement for one night. That can keep for another time." I picked up the plates and carried them to the kitchen.

"Then, I'll see you tomorrow?"

"Of course," I said, seeing her to the door.

As I placed the plates and coffee cups in the dishwasher, my mind whirled—a live-streamed show of the pastor opening the safe deposit box. The possibility was intriguing and would appeal to thousands, maybe millions. And what other charity had the opportunity to reach such a broad audience? The more I reflected on Rachel's vision, the more I liked the idea. But I wanted Connor's opinion and for him to point out the downside of the event. There was always a downside to every event, even if it was minute.

When Connor came home, I pulled him onto the couch in the sunroom. He wrapped his arm around me as I told him of Rachel's idea.

"It sounds wonderful, honey, but you'd need an army to pull this off—marketing people, IT people for the website and ticket sales, someone to handle the media, and more. It wouldn't be like your community quilt or Christmas craft shows. This could be huge. And you don't even know if this pastor is capable or wants to come to the studio. Maybe he's too old or doesn't want to be part of this kind of event. And the others you've spoken to. Would they be willing to tell their story on camera? Then there's the stress. More than anything, I'd be worried you wouldn't be able to handle the event and your pregnancy at the same time."

"I know. There's a lot to think about. But Rachel's handled significant events such as this or knows people who have. Maybe it wouldn't be as overwhelming as we think if we hired an event firm to handle all the details."

"All it takes is money." Connor held up his hand and rubbed his thumb and fingers together.

"Yeah, but Rachel's great at getting sponsors, and the reward could be amazing." I looked at him with raised brows. "Think about how many dogs could be adopted, and we could expand Archie's helpline and our contributions to other charities."

"The possibility is exciting, but let's think about it a bit more. Besides, you haven't even talked to the pastor or the other relatives. You don't know what their stories are. Why not complete those interviews first, then revisit the big event topic?"

"You're right. First things first. But as soon as I finish the interviews, I plan to give Rachel the go-ahead to start looking into the logistics on how to pull off the project. Now, how was your trip to West Palm? Did you enjoy your time with Cathy and Seth? How are they doing?" I gazed at Connor's profile in anticipation of his response.

"Cathy's done a great job fixing up the apartment, and she seems to love living in West Palm Beach and being near the ocean."

"You know that's not what I meant. How are she and Seth doing?" I leaned my head onto his shoulder.

"Every relationship has its adjustment period. They've only been with each other for a few months. I think it's too soon to tell."

"Well, I hope Seth didn't jump too quickly. Your sister can be a handful."

"What? You experienced that first hand, did you?" asked Connor, tongue in cheek.

I didn't need to say a word. Connor was well aware I'd run into Cathy's prickly personality during her stay at the cottage over Christmas.

"I'm sure they'll be fine. Look at us?" said Connor. "We haven't known each other that long, and now we're married with two kids on the way." He kissed my forehead

Seth and Cathy didn't have what Connor and I did, but I prayed their relationship would last.

Chapter 15

A few days later, Leslie and I met to discuss what we'd found out about the contacts we'd made with the relatives of the three men. As usual, she had prepared tea and a plate of cookies to nibble on while we talked in her kitchen. Before we got started, I told her about Rachel's idea to live stream the opening of the safe deposit box. She was all for the big event and vividly remembered sitting in front of the TV as Geraldo Rivera opened the vault.

"It was the most exciting event we'd seen on TV. Everyone was talking about it," she said.

"We can't even consider Rachel's plan until we hear what the other relatives have to say. You go first. What about Bob Hanley?" I sipped my tea and bit into a cookie.

"Okay," said Leslie. Her eyes sparkled, and her enthusiasm overflowed. "First, I spoke with the son of the pilot. What a story! His father was only seventeen when he started flying contraband liquor from the Bahamas into Miami for Capone."

"What? He wasn't even out of high school. How'd he get hooked up with such a high-profile person?" I couldn't believe such a young man would be introduced to the gangster, let alone fly a plane for him.

"I'm not going to tell you," Leslie said smugly. "I'll let Hanley's son do that. But believe me when I say, this story is as fantastic as Thelma's."

"I take it that means we need to go down and meet the son in Hollywood."

"Actually, I asked if he would be willing to come up to the studio and be videotaped telling us the story. He agreed." Leslie sat back, a smile of satisfaction on her face.

"You're a genius. But I guess that means no lunch on the boardwalk." I stuck out my lower lip in a pout. I was looking forward to the road trip.

"Not this time. Bob's son said his father wrote his memoirs, and there are several chapters about his time flying for Capone. The son's name is Frank Hanley, and this is his contact number so you can schedule the taping." Leslie handed me the information.

"A gold mine," I said, clutching the paper to my chest. "What about John Orr Sr.?"

"Well, his granddaughter told me a tragic story about Mr. Orr and Capone. She also faxed over a couple of old newspaper clippings that pretty much describe the account. Here they are." Leslie pushed the pages across the table to me.

I scanned them.

"Oh my gosh. This is terrible!" I was astonished by what I read—Capone's thugs had assaulted Mr. Orr.

"Yes. It's the first time we've run across Capone's blatant use of force," said Leslie.

"Do you think the granddaughter would be willing to talk on camera?" One of the keys to our success, if we were to move forward with the lockbox special, would be the stories told by the relatives of those on the key tags.

"I didn't ask her, but I can't image she'd say 'no.' She seemed most anxious to tell her grandfather's story."

"Great."

We now had two people we could tape. Oh, how I wished we'd recorded Thelma's account of her time with Capone. We had to get that story on tape. Perhaps we could get that before too long.

"Your turn," said Leslie. "How'd it go with Pastor Pearson?"

"It's kind of a funny story," I said with a chuckle.

"How so?" Leslie folded her arms on the table and leaned in.

"Nope. That one will remain a secret until I can arrange for someone up where he's living to videotape him."

"Is he mobile, and would he consent to open the safe deposit box on live TV?"

"I didn't ask him since we haven't decided to do it. If we decide to move ahead with the opening, I'll explain everything to him and pop the question." I gathered my things and got ready to leave. "Has David gotten back to you yet? You haven't said much about him lately regarding these names."

"I forgot to tell you. All the names are on the Florida list."

"That's good news, isn't it? So why do you look so glum?" I asked.

"He wants to come to the house." Leslie's gaze fell to her lap.

"How do you feel about that? About him?"

"I like David. I want us to continue to enjoy each other's company. But moving these boxes is going to be a huge change for me. I don't know if I'm up to it." Her shoulders drooped.

"This was going to happen eventually. I guess it's time we organize your boxes. I'll get Connor right on it." I hugged Leslie before leaving.

Connor and I sat at the kitchen island and enjoyed a bowl of fruit while I explained Leslie's project.

"My assignment doesn't start for another two weeks. I'll go over to Leslie's tomorrow and assess the situation. If there's enough space, I'll reorganize the rooms with shelving, and we can restack the containers there. If it looks like too many boxes, I'll see about a storage shed."

"Believe me, it's more than a one-man job. You'll need help moving the boxes out to put shelves in the room and then moving them back in. And don't be shocked when you see her home. I guarantee you've never seen anything like it."

"Well, we'll get her fixed up so she can receive David. I wouldn't want the containers to prevent her from filling her life with love." Connor winked and gave me one of his characteristic grins.

"You, Mr. Romero, are my Prince Charming and soon to be Leslie's hero."

"I'd better stay your Prince Charming, or you'll be in big trouble." Connor's eyes absorbed mine as he took my hand and kissed the back.

~

On Friday, Frank Hanley came to the studio where I had it set up like a living room—chair, coffee table, small area rug. Two cameras would video him from the side and front. The communications students from the high school were on hand to handle the cameras and audio.

I met Frank at the door. Of medium build, he wore casual clothes, and his lively hazel eyes made him appear a young mid-sixty. We shook hands, and he handed me his signed consent form along with several printed photos of his father.

"Thank you so much for coming up to the studio and for the images. Your father's experience with Al Capone is quite a story." I led him to the set and gestured for him to sit.

"Leslie said something about a project you're working on."

"She and I are working on a history project that involves your father and several others from Capone's past that were friends or acquaintances of his. Since we weren't acquainted with any of these individuals, we decided to learn their stories by contacting their relatives."

"How'd you get my father's name?" Frank folded his hands in his lap.

"We found it on a piece of paper that may have been associated with Capone. I hired a genealogist to see if we could find your father's children or relatives. That's how we found you." I sat in a chair outside the camera shot to prompt Frank with questions, if necessary.

"How do you intend to use this video?"

"Right now, we just want it for historical purposes. The consent form you signed gives you the option to agree or deny permission should we plan to put it on air. I hope you're comfortable with that."

"I am."

"I don't want to take up too much of your time, so I'd like you to relax and think of this seating area like your living room. The conversation can be that casual. Please introduce yourself, tell us a little about your time in Florida, and your occupation. Then tell us the entire story of how your father met Al Capone and began flying illicit liquor into Miami for him."

Frank adjusted himself in the chair, leaned back, and placed his elbows comfortably on the chair arms. Having worked with the camera persons before, the camera crew understood when to start the cameras rolling.

"I'm Frank Hanley, son of Robert Hanley. I was born in Hollywood, Florida, and have lived there all my life. I worked in the logistics business until I retired. Now I work with nonprofits to help them find transportation connections to fly medicines and donations into countries suffering from natural disasters."

"You're doing great, Frank. Now, tell us about your father."

~

Miami 1927

Robert "Bob" Hanley adjusted his black bowtie in the mirror before going out onto the floor. Even though he was a busboy and one of the low men on the restaurant totem pole, he wanted to look good in the upscale Miami restaurant. Bussing tables was his part-time job, and he couldn't afford to lose it. Being able to pay for his flying lessons depended upon it.

He meandered through the tables with his tray, stopped at a four-top, and began transferring used drinking glasses and plates onto his tray.

"Hey, kid, don't I know you? Aren't you Sonny's classmate?"

Bob turned to see Sonny's father sitting at the next table with two other hefty men. Even though he and Sonny were both seniors at St. Patrick Catholic School on Miami Beach and had attended several school and social functions together, Bob had never met Sonny's father. But he knew who the man was. Everyone knew who he was—Al Capone, Chicago's number one gangster.

"Yes, sir. Nice to see you." Bob stood straight, hoping his nervousness didn't cause his voice to shake.

"Sonny tells me you're a pilot. That so?" Capone's penetrating eyes gazed at Bob as though he was looking right through him.

"Yes, sir. I've been taking flying lessons. Had my first solo flight a couple of weeks ago."

"You a good pilot?" Capone didn't blink as he waited for an answer.

"Yes, sir. Haven't crashed yet."

Capone looked at his men, then let out a hearty laugh. His men followed suit. "That's funny, kid. Very funny. I guess if you had crashed, you wouldn't be here now. Right?"

"Yes, sir," said Bob, giving Capone a half-smile and wondering if he shouldn't just pick up his tray and hustle back to the kitchen and out the door.

"How'd you like to fly for me on the weekends? Bring some cargo over from the Bahamas to Miami? Make three hundred big ones a trip?"

Bob couldn't believe his ears. Three hundred dollars just to fly from the Bahamas to Miami? His dream was to find a job flying once he was out of school. This opportunity could give him the experience he needed and make his dream come true.

"I'd have to check with my parents," said Bob.

Capone rose and walked over to the young man. He put his arm around the kid's shoulders and spoke in a low voice.

"Uh, this isn't the kind of job your parents would approve of, kid. I need an answer, and I need it now. I got cargo to move."

Bob didn't take long to answer. He was seventeen, almost eighteen, and needed to start making his own decisions.

"Yes, sir. I'll take it."

"Good decision," said Capone. He shook Bob's hand and handed him a folded piece of paper. "See this man at this address and tell him who you are. He'll give you a schedule and all the information you'll need. Just do what he tells you."

Bob unfolded the paper and nodded.

Though Bob never saw Capone again, that one meeting was enough to get him hauling illegal booze into Biscayne Bay on weekends.

Robert told his folks he was staying with his buddy in Hollywood fifteen miles to his north for the weekend. Then, on Friday afternoons after school, he'd catch a ferry over to West End in the Bahamas. There, he'd pick up the plane, which was already loaded with crates of liquor, and fly it into Biscayne Bay. A couple of trips a night, he'd pocket $600 in cash. On any given weekend, he'd pick up anywhere from $1200-$1800. With a shoebox overflowing with money, the young pilot stashed much of it under his mattress. To make sure his mother was none the wiser, he resorted to doing his own laundry, including making his own bed.

The fact that he'd never flown at night before scared the willy out of Bob on his first flight, but other pilots on this haul helped him navigate the 100 miles. After a few trips, it was a piece of cake. Everything worked fine until one night.

"You're all loaded and ready to go," said Manuel to Bob as he closed the cargo door of the plane sitting next to the loading dock on West End.

"See you in a couple of hours," said Bob.

The night was clear as he flew his single-engine Commandaire biplane on floats from the isle of Grand Bahama to Biscayne Bay, landed the plane, and taxied toward the pick-up point. Keeping the plane idling, he closed his eyes and leaned back against his seat as Capone's men unloaded the contraband into waiting trucks. All of a sudden, there was a flurry of noise and activity.

"We've been spotted!" yelled one of the men. "Get going! Get outta here!"

The man slammed the plane's cargo door shut, and Bob taxied into the bay. He'd just taken off when he caught sight of the Coast Guard Cutter approach on the starboard side. He could have easily made it out to sea, but his young macho ego grabbed that part of him that liked to thumb its nose at authority.

"Let's see what you guys do with this young ace," Bob said out loud above the roar of the plane's engine. He adjusted his leather helmet and goggles, threw the ends of his scarf around his neck, and banked the plane toward the cutter.

"Yahoo!" he yelled like a cowboy on a bronco as he buzzed the plane over the cutter.

Pulling the plane up, the unmistakable rat-a-tat-tat of a machine gun resounded in Bob's ears. A barrage of bullets whizzed by, one hitting the belly of the aircraft.

Seering pain immediately shot through Bob's right leg as though a hot poker had stabbed his flesh. He leaned forward and put his hand into his boot. When he withdrew it, his hand was wet. Turning on his flashlight, he gasped when he saw his pant leg saturated in blood.

"Oh, God! Oh, God! Please save me," he pleaded.

Bob felt woozy, as though he would faint, and guided the plane toward the water.

Then all went black.

When Bob's parents learned he wasn't in school on Monday morning, an all-out search ensued. Bob's girlfriend, the daughter of a customs agent, informed Bob's parents the Coast Guard had shot him down. She suggested they speak with Capone.

Once informed, the head of The Outfit spared no expense in trying to find his downed pilot. Bob was finally located unconscious in a mangrove swamp miles from West End. He was transported by speed boat to Capone's secret base, an old concrete ship called 'Sappona' marooned just off Bimini. There, a doctor patched him up.

Walking on crutches, Bob returned to school a hero of sorts. In the hallways, classmates bombarded him with questions about his adventure.

"Hey, Robert, what's it like being a rumrunner?"

"Weren't you scared?"

"How'd you like working for Al Capone?"

"What's he like?"

After recovering from his harrowing experience, Bob continued to run booze for Capone for another two years. Proceeds from his short but lucrative career allowed him to purchase a car and pay for his college education.

~

Leslie was right. Frank's story of his father's experience with Capone was just as exciting as Thelma's.

I leaned forward. "What happened to your father? Did he ever live his dream of becoming a commercial pilot?"

"Dad eventually opened a small charter plane business. Even though he was breaking the law and working for a ruthless man, Dad was grateful for his experience during the Prohibition era. If it hadn't been for his flying job with Capone, he would never have experienced night flying and all that goes along with getting out of difficult situations." Frank rose to leave.

"Frank, one last question, if I may. Did you ever run into a man by the name of Derick Eastway? He lived in Deerfield Beach."

"Hmm. I'm not familiar with the name," he said.

"Well, Leslie and I can't thank you enough for coming up and sharing your father's story. We'll be in touch as this project moves forward." I walked Frank to the door. "You know, you should publish your father's memoirs. That story alone is priceless."

"Perhaps someday," said Frank.

I hoped he didn't wait too long.

On Saturday morning, Leslie, Connor, David, and I gathered in the sunroom to share Bob Hanley's video with them. I served tea and danish.

"Quite the story," said Connor when the video ended.

"Can you imagine a seventeen-year-old having that kind of adventure and living to tell about it? How exciting! It would make a great movie," Leslie said.

"All the stories are good, but I can't help thinking about what Mrs. Eastway said about believing her husband was killed because of the lockbox." I closed out the video and my laptop.

"Do you know how he died?" David's gaze bobbed between Leslie and me.

"Come to think of it, we don't know anything about his official cause of death. Because we already have our hands full trying to get the relative's stories, I never thought to delve into that mystery, too."

"Let Connor and me work on that," said David. "Since I've finished with the banks and we know everyone on the list has something in the Florida repository, I'm free to turn my attention to something else. What about it, Connor?"

Leslie and I shot Connor a "don't you dare" look. He'd committed his time to work on Leslie's hoard of boxes.

"I'd love to," said Connor. "But I've got an assignment in two weeks, and I'm committed to a project here until then. I'll be glad to act as a consultant, but you'll have to fly solo on this one, David. Sorry."

"No problem," he said. "I'll get started on Monday."

"In case you need a resource, here's contact info for a Boca Raton homicide detective. He's worked with us on our other cases and may be able to help you since he works closely with the Deerfield Beach officers at the Broward Sheriff's Office. Also, let me also give you Mrs. Easway's contact info. She may be able to shed more light on this." I texted David and sent him both John Kester's and Mrs. Eastway's phone numbers.

"One cause of death and anything else I can discover coming right up," said David.

Chapter 16

"You weren't kidding when you said Leslie's project was a two-person job. Both the fellow I hired to help me and I are pooped." Connor sat on a stool at the kitchen island and took off his cap. His wet hair was plastered to his head, and his T-shirt was stained with sweat.

"So, how are you going to turn her containers into an organized collection of history?" I set a bottle of Gatorade before him.

"I've got some ideas that I've discussed with her and will get started tomorrow on the build-out. Until I can get the shelves installed, the containers are in a U-Haul in her driveway. I hope the neighbors won't think she's moving." Connor took two large gulps of his drink.

"Do you think you'll be able to finish by the time you leave for your assignment?" I tossed lettuce into a bowl and started slicing cucumbers, red peppers, celery, and tomatoes to go with it. I'd add the shrimp just before we sat down to eat.

"It'll be a challenge, that's for sure." He drained the rest of his Gatorade. "I'll go take a shower and be back for dinner."

My phone rang while mixing the red wine vinegar, sugar, oil, and pepper for our salad dressing.

"Randi Brooks," I said.

"Miss Brooks, this is Cameron Trask of Lady Lake, Florida. I wanted you to know I've finished the videotaping of Reverend Lester Pearson. I've sent you a link so you can download it."

"Great, I'll watch it tonight, and thanks for doing this on such short notice. With the elderly, time is of the essence, as you can imagine." I sprinkled the dressing on the salad.

"Don't I know. My grandma is in her mid-eighties, and I'm just hearing some of her wonderful stories for the first time. I'm taping them for my children. Times were so different then," he said.

"Well, thanks for your time, Cameron, and send me an invoice. I'll take care of it tomorrow."

"You got it. By the way, the Reverend has a pretty fascinating story about his father. I had to laugh at the punchline."

I pulled up. "What do you mean?"

"Oh, no. I'm not going to give it away. You'll find out. Let me know if I can help you again."

After dinner, I once again invited Leslie to sit down with Connor and me to view the video narrated by the Reverend.

~

Miami 1929

Dr. Homer Pearson settled onto the couch after dinner and lit his pipe. *The blue haze of cherry tobacco curled into the room, permeating the air with a sweet aroma. The doctor's wife, Abigail, joined him on the couch. She brought the new Miami phone directory and opened it to the Ps. She pointed to the page.*

"See. There we are. One of the newest listings in the directory. This should help get our practice on a sure footing. With the growing community, we're certain to grow right along with it." Abigail smiled warmly at her husband.

Homer and Abigail had moved to Miami from Blairsville, Georgia, a small community in the northwest corner of the state not far from the North Carolina border. They had loved the rural community, but both longed for a much larger city where they would be needed. Plus, they wanted to settle in a warmer climate closer to the ocean. When they heard Miami was one of the fastest-growing communities in the south, they decided to pull up stakes and take their chances. So far, they hadn't regretted their decision.

Homer put down his pipe and lifted his tumbler of scotch and soda. Despite Prohibition, illegal liquor was readily available in most parts of Miami if he knew the right people. He did. It was a gift from one of his satisfied patients. He drank the scotch sparingly.

Just as they were settling comfortably on the couch, the phone rang. As always, Abigail answered.

"Hello? Why, yes. This is Dr. Pearson's residence. Just a minute." Abigail looked at her husband with a furrowed brow and closed her hand over the receiver. "It's for you. He sounds very rough."

Homer rose and accepted the receiver from his wife. "Dr. Pearson...Yes...Urgent?--I'll come right over...Oh, *you'll send a car?...I'm to wait for you out front." Homer hung up.*

"Who was that?" asked Abigail.

"I don't really know. He seemed a bit mysterious but said he needed a doctor now. That it was urgent. Said he'd send a car for me." Homer walked into the foyer, plucked his jacket from the coat stand, and put it on. Then he grabbed his bag.

"He didn't say what the issue was or where he lived?"

"No. Didn't even tell me what the symptoms were. He simply said he'd send a driver to pick me up. Must be someone pretty important."

"Or someone who has a condition he doesn't want anyone else to know about. Maybe you shouldn't go. All this seems pretty suspicious to me."

"I've got to go, Abigail. That's what doctors do— make house calls to care for those that need them. I'll be fine." Homer kissed Abigail's forehead and walked out the front door. He waited for the car at the curb.

Ten minutes later, a shiny black car pulled up in front of Dr. Pearson's home. A large man with a pockmarked face got out, walked around the car, and opened the back door. "Dr. Pearson?" he asked in a deep, gruff voice. Dr. Pearson nodded.

As Homer sat in the car's well-appointed back seat—black leather upholstery and polished maple—he wondered where he was going. Once the vehicle started onto the MacArthur Causeway, he knew he was headed for Miami Beach. He didn't know anyone there. It was an island of expensive hotels, homes, and entertainment venues. He'd been there for dinner but hadn't been in Miami long enough to make friends with those that lived across Biscayne Bay.

Before they got halfway across the bridge, the car took a left onto Palm Island. The few houses he passed were impressive—enormous with lush, tropical, perfectly landscaped yards. The vehicle stopped at a two-story building with a double wooden gate—93 Palm Island. The driver honked, the gate opened, and the car pulled onto a circular driveway. He car stopped in front of the house.

"Go on up to the door. Someone will greet you," said the driver.

Homer got out and walked to the door, tightly clutching his medical bag. Before he had an opportunity to knock, a man stepped into the threshold.

"This way," he said without introducing himself.

Homer followed the man with broad shoulders down a long hallway, up a flight of stairs, and into a well-appointed sitting room adjacent to a bedroom. The patient was lying on a red velvet couch, eyes closed, a patchwork quilt pulled up to his chin.

"Boss, the doc's here," said the man in a soft voice, as though speaking to a child.

The boss groaned and opened his eyes.

Homer pulled a matching velvet ottoman close to the couch and sat. He took out his stethoscope and draped it about his neck. Then he withdrew a thermometer. Looking into the glassy eyes of the patient, he pulled back as he recognized the man—Al Capone.

He knew Capone lived in Miami Beach. He'd seen the photos in the newspaper, read the scathing articles. But never in a million years did he think he'd ever run into the notorious gangster, let alone treat him as a patient.

"Open your mouth, please." Homer shook down the mercury in the glass thermometer with trembling hands and then stuck the device into Capone's mouth. He looked at his watch, waiting for the required three minutes to pass. He

removed the thermometer, read the temperature—102—and shook the thermometer down. He cleaned it with alcohol, then returned the device to his bag.

Next, he brought out a small flashlight. He lifted Capone's eyelids, one after the other, and checked his pupils. Then his pulse.

"I need to listen to your chest." He unbuttoned Capone's striped pajamas. With the listening device's earpieces to his ears, he placed the resonator on the man's chest. "Deep breaths, please. Can you sit up?" Homer helped Capone do so, then put the stethoscope on his back. "Deep breaths." Homer returned his equipment to his bag.

"What is it, Doc?" asked Capone in a weak raspy voice. He looked at the doctor through half-closed eyelids.

"The good news is your lungs are clear. The bad news is you have the flu. Unfortunately, there's not much we can do about that. Take aspirin, rest, drink plenty of fluids, and don't overexert yourself. It should subside in a few days."

"That's all?"

"There's no magic pill, I'm afraid," said Homer.

"Well, thanks, Doc." Capone rolled over and closed his eyes.

Homer retraced his steps to the front door, followed by a bodyguard. Before he left, Capone's man handed him a one hundred dollar bill.

"Well, who was it?" asked Abigail when Homer returned.

"You won't believe me," said Homer.

"Was it the man's pregnant wife? Or was it a pregnant lover? Maybe a girlfriend or daughter?"

"None of the above," said Homer. "It was Al Capone."

Abigail inhaled sharply. "Al Capone! The gangster?"

"Yep. He has the flu."

"But, Homer, why did he call you? You're not an internist or family doctor. You're an OB/GYN."

~

Leslie, Connor, and I looked at each other and couldn't help but laugh.

"An OB/GYN treating Capone for the flu? Now I've heard everything. I'll bet that was the most interesting patient Dr. Pearson ever had," said Leslie.

"At least he lived to talk about it." I closed down the computer.

"Well, I'm going to bed, ladies. I had a long day today and have a lot to do tomorrow. I'll see you in the morning, Leslie." Connor got up, kissed us both goodnight on the cheek, and walked toward the stairs.

"How are you feeling about what Connor's doing?" I asked Leslie.

"It's different, but I'm warming up to it. I'm sure when he's through, everything will be nice and orderly. But I just won't know what to do with all the space." Leslie's eyes narrowed, and her face looked pinched.

"We'll fill it with some interesting furniture so you and David can sit on a couch together. What you do after that is up to you." I gazed at Leslie and wiggled my eyebrows.

"Oh!" Leslie shot me a sheepish grin.

I walked her home, then stayed up and contemplated our last interview—John Orr's granddaughter. Having seen or met the relatives of those whose names were on the key tags, I couldn't imagine any of them playing a role in Derick Eastway's death. But I needed to wait and see what David turned up.

Over the next few mornings, I hardly made my way to the bathroom before morning sickness took hold of me big time. I'd been fine up to now, at least able to handle the slight nausea and fatigue, but its full force was now upon me. Saltines. Ice cream. Lemons. Bananas. I tried them all and finally found the combination that worked for me—watermelon and peppermint. Not necessarily eaten together. Connor fixed a container of cut-up watermelon and a baggie with peppermint sticks. This way, I could snack while at the studio.

Rachel got to work on my old room—removing the furniture and having the walls painted, laying new flooring, and installing blinds. Every day I came home to something new and exciting. Soon, the room would have furniture and look like an actual guest room, and one day a child's room instead of a high school girl's memories.

For the twin's nursery, we were waiting to know their gender before upgrading. Except for the furniture we ordered to fit either gender, we didn't know what to do. Once again, Rachel pulled some designs together. Both rooms would be finished at the same time in a few weeks.

I contacted Emily Thompson, Robert Orr Sr.'s granddaughter, the following week. She was eager to right the wrong her grandfather had experienced at the hands of Capone so many years ago. And although she could offer no more information than the newspaper articles Mandy sent us, she could relate how her family suffered after her grandfather's death. Once again, I located a local videographer and set up the interview. I anticipated this interview to be quite emotional.

~

I received the keys back from Curtis and returned them to the lockbox, leaving key number nine the only one we couldn't locate. I also placed copies of Curtis's report in the box and the list we made of the keys. As I put the lockbox in the locked file cabinet in the den, I heard the shrill train whistle. Looking into my phone, I saw it was David. I opened the gate and went to the door.

"Please come in. What brings you by?"

"I'm so sorry to come without calling first, but I just had to let you know as soon as possible." His gaze dropped, and his face creased in worry.

"Whatever is wrong?" I led David into the sunroom, where we sat.

"Mrs. Eastway is dead."

I jumped up. "Dead? How'd you find out?" This was not good news. We were getting to the end of the interviews, and we'd needed to speak with her.

"Derick was a large benefactor of the Friends of Deerfield Island Park. The president of the organization just emailed the members that Mrs. Eastway passed away last night."

"How horrible. Do you know how she died?"

Was her death a broken heart from losing her husband? Natural causes? Something else, like foul play or, perhaps, alcoholism? She did initially come to Boca Grande with alcohol on her breath.

"That wasn't mentioned in the email, but it did say her home was ransacked, as though it was a robbery. Certainly is curious that her husband should die with her convinced the lockbox had something to do with it, and now she's dead as well. Makes you wonder if there's any truth to what she believed."

"But who would know about the lockbox beside us? And we haven't told any of those we interviewed about it."

"Now that I think about it, anyone who read Capone's niece's book would know about the lockbox, but I doubt anyone knew that Derick found it except his wife and, of course, us."

"And Rachel," I said. "But she knows not to breathe a word to anyone.

"But what if the person who went through Mrs. Eastway's house found out she gave the lockbox to you? Wouldn't that put a target on your back?"

I paced the room. "I think we need to tell Connor about this. He's over at Leslie's helping her with a project."

"Can't we just go over there?" David rose and started for the back door.

"No!" I said, grabbing his arm.

He stopped cold.

"I'm sorry, David, I didn't mean to be so forceful. It's just that Connor's helping Leslie with a bit of a...umm...sensitive project she doesn't want anyone to see until it's complete. It's better that I call them." I pulled out my phone.

"Hey, honey, how's it going?—Great. David's here and needs to see both you and Leslie. He says it's important...Okay, see you soon." I hung up. "They'll be here in a few minutes. Something to drink?" I went to the kitchen, poured four glasses of iced tea, and took them to the sunroom. As I set them down, Connor and Leslie entered through the back door.

"Okay, what's so important?" Connor asked. His T-shirt and shorts were blotched with sweat.

David greeted Leslie with a hug and kiss on the cheek. Then we all sat while he explained to Connor and Leslie about the email he'd received.

"Oh, my," said Leslie, slapping her cheeks. "We now have two people who died because of the lockbox?"

"Hold on. Just because Mr. and Mrs. Eastway died doesn't mean it has to do with the lockbox. David, you were looking into Derick's death. What did you find out about that?" asked Connor, always Mr. Practical.

"Eastway died in his workroom, the cause of death listed as a heart attack, though there were signs of a struggle, and he had a contusion on his head. Of course, stress is a major cause of heart attacks, but the fact that he may have been hit over the head adds a suspicious element. According to his neighbors, he was typically an easy-going person, but he seemed nervous and jittery right before he died. They didn't know why."

"Did anyone mention the lockbox?" I asked.

"No. And I didn't bring it up. I did speak with the officer who was on the scene. He was waiting for the autopsy to confirm foul play, but he did say that it appeared someone must have been looking for something as his workroom was in total disarray."

Leslie gasped. "The same as Mrs. Eastway's home when they found her."

"It does seem odd that both of them would die surrounded by disorder. That's too much of a coincidence for me. I wonder if the police noticed the similarity?" I asked.

"If different officers worked the crime scenes, they might not realize the parallel. Perhaps Kester could contact the Broward County Sheriffs Office in Deerfield and suggest they dig a bit deeper," said Connor.

"I'll call him tomorrow and see what he says. Of course, I'll have to tell him the entire story of the lockbox." I knew Kester would roll his eyes at me for having gotten involved in another caper, even though he'd find it as fascinating as I had.

"Yeah, but at least he'd be alerted that you might be in danger again since you now have the lockbox," said David.

We all fell silent and looked at each other.

"Look, I'll take care of Randi," said Connor. "All we have to go on so far is coincidence and conjecture. We don't know how Mrs. Eastway died. Perhaps if Kester could inquire while talking with the Deerfield station, we'd have more to go on. In the meantime, everyone continues with their daily routines."

David spoke to Leslie a few minutes, then Connor escorted her back to her house to finish his work on her rooms. I walked David to the door.

"There are still a couple of things I want to look into. I'll get back to you when I have more answers," he said before leaving.

After he left, I closed the front gate, set the alarm, and stood there bewildered. I hoped I wouldn't run into another lunatic like James Carl when I uncovered the stolen statues.

As I walked back through the house, I noticed Bigfoot lying on his side on the kitchen floor, pawing at the bottom of the island.

"What are you doing, my friend? You lose something under there?" I gently pushed him aside and looked where he was pawing. The tiniest corner of something shiny poked out from under the island. The object was so small, I couldn't get my fingers on it. "Be right back," I said to Bigfoot. He swished his tail and returned to pawing at the object.

I rushed upstairs and pulled a pair of tweezers from my cosmetic bag. Scooting Bigfoot aside again, I pinched the object's corner and tugged. A plastic bag emerged. Key number nine!

Thinking back to how this could have happened, I remembered that when I tried to get all the bags back into the lockbox, they slid off the counter and onto the floor.

Number nine must have slipped beneath the counter in my haste to pick them up.

"You're the hero once again, big guy. Thanks for finding it." I lifted Bigfoot and kissed his head. "Good job!" He gave me a smug look.

Tomorrow, I'd pack up the baggie and send the key to Curtis. Perhaps it was the clue we were looking for.

Chapter 17

After taking the package with key number nine to the post office in the morning, I put in a call to Kester.

"Hey, Randi. How's the married lady? Or should I say, mother to be?"

"She's doing great. How's my favorite detective and rescuer of women in distress?" After being involved with several of my earlier escapades and rescuing me from what could have been life-threatening situations, he was my favored champion.

"Let's see. You've started this conversation by flattering me, so I guess that means you're working on another mystery and need my assistance."

"Only if you want to prevent another ominous circumstance." I left out the crucial parts to whet his appetite.

"Okay, I'm hooked. Where are we meeting for lunch this time?"

"Actually, I need you to come by Boca Grande. I'm fixing lunch, and I want to show you something. Connor will be home from working at Leslie's, and he'll join us. How's noon?"

"You know I can't say 'no' to you. And the fact that Connor will be there helped me make up my mind. It'll be nice to see the new groom and father-to-be. Twins! That's amazing. See you then."

I phoned Connor to let him know about our lunch date and asked him to invite Leslie. She wanted to stay at her house and go through some of her boxes, so lunch would be just the three of us. Kester arrived with a warm peck on my cheek and a manly hug for Connor.

"I can't believe that in a few months, you two will have babies in your arms."

Connor and I looked at each other.

"We can't believe it either, but the reality is hitting close to home these days" I pointed to my baby bump that was expanding every day.

"It's been a long time since I held a baby, but you know you can count on Adele and me to babysit when you're ready to leave the kids and take an afternoon or night for yourselves."

"Said with a generous heart until you have to take care of two squealing kids at the same time with poop in their diapers," said Connor with a laugh.

"You two go sit in the sunroom, and I'll get the item I want Kester to see." I went to the den to retrieve the lockbox and put the opened rusted container on the coffee table.

Kester looked at the box curiously. "What are those? Safe deposit keys?" He picked up a baggie and examined the contents.

"Here's the background," I said. I explained to Kester how I came into the possession of the lockbox and what we'd done so far regarding the investigation.

"That's quite a yarn," he said, drawing his hand through his thinning hair. "So you think this lockbox had something to do with the Eastways' deaths?"

"Mrs. Eastway claimed her husband's death was tied to the lockbox. According to the autopsy, Mr. Eastway died of a heart attack, but it also looked like he'd been hit over the head. And the interesting thing is the way both he and his wife died amidst a background of chaos. Both crime scenes were as though someone was looking for something. With Mrs. Eastway, the house was in shambles, like a robbery gone bad," I said.

"If two different officers investigated the crimes, we're afraid they might not realize the significance of the two crime scenes," said Connor. "And, of course, they don't know about the lockbox."

"So, what do you want me to do?" Kester peeked at us over the top of his glasses.

"Perhaps you could give them a call, you know, as a professional courtesy and let them know you received a tip that the two crimes might be connected. That an item in the deceased's possession may have been the catalyst for their deaths," I said.

"And when they ask me what that item might be, what am I supposed to tell them?" Kester sat back and crossed his arms.

"Tell them you're not at liberty to say right now, as the tipster came to you in confidence because his life may be in danger." I gave Kester a stern stare.

"And just how do you figure that?" Kester's gaze vacillated between Connor and me.

"The perp may have coerced Sheila Eastway into telling him it's now in my possession," I said.

Kester got up and paced the room. "Geez, Randi. Here we go again."

"I'll keep Randi safe," said Connor. "The only hitch is I have an assignment for a couple of weeks."

"I forgot all about your assignment. How can you even consider going with a killer on the loose?" I gazed at Connor in astonishment.

I'd been in this position before with someone looking for me. Once when Raul, the man who killed my parents, was on the loose and heading back to Florida, and when James Carl was looking to silence me before I found the stolen statues. Being pursued was an uncomfortable situation to be in.

"Honey, don't you think you're overreacting? We don't even know if there is a killer on the loose. If there is, there's no proof he knows you have the lockbox," said Connor.

"When's the assignment?" asked Kester

"Starting next week," Connor said.

Kester ran his hand down his face. "First, let me talk to the Broward Sheriff's Office in Deerfield. If it looks like there's even an inkling of possibility that the crimes are connected, I'll let you know."

"And if there is, I'll cancel my assignment," said Connor. He pulled me close and sealed his commitment with a kiss to my temple.

"Even if there's no connection, I'll talk to Adele. Maybe she and I can move into the guesthouse while you're away," said Kester

"That would make both of us feel far more comfortable knowing you would be here, especially at night." Connor squeezed my hand.

"Okay, let me see what I can find out, but if I can't get anywhere without divulging the story of the lockbox, then I'll need to share it. That's not negotiable." Kester gave both Connor and me a piercing stare. "Just understand, I'll be asking in an unofficial capacity. They'll have no obligation to tell me anything."

"Understood," Connor and I said in unison.

With that taken care of, we went into the kitchen. I served lunch while we sat at the island and talked about life. Afterward, I went back to the studio to finish up some projects. While there, the videographer I'd contacted sent me an email with a link to Orr's granddaughter's account of what happened to him.

Later that night, Connor, Leslie, and I sat in the sunroom and listened to the interview.

~

Miami 1930

Dr. Samuel Willard gazed with deep concern at his friend and patient, John B. "Jack" Orr Sr., Miami Beach's celebrated builder, beloved philanthropist, and civic supporter. A Scottish mason, he'd apprenticed in Glasgow, Scotland, from 1901 to 1906 before arriving in Miami to work his trade. He built the Biltmore Estate, the Olympia Theater, Viscaya, and several other monuments and buildings around Miami. He lived on Palm Island, just two lots down from Capone.

"I wish you'd reconsider, Jack. Your recent operations followed by long illnesses have left you quite frail. Don't add the stress of heading up such an endeavor on top of these medical issues. I'm afraid it will push your

172

system to the brink." Dr. Willard looked at his friend with concern.

Jack placed a delicate hand—nothing but skin and bones—on the doctor's shoulder and patted it. Then he spoke in as strong a voice as he could muster.

"I appreciate your concern, Sam, but I can't let the community I love fall farther into chaos. For years, gambling, prostitution, illegal liquor, and corruption at every level have turned Maimi Beach into an immoral environment. It's affecting our quality of life. It's affecting the quality of life of our children and grandchildren. It's time we admitted complicity in destroying our treasured city and what we came here for in the first place—a decent life. It's time we did something about cleaning up the place."

The fact was, Miami Beach had been corrupt for decades. Even when Dade County was declared dry in 1913, illicit booze saturated the county long before National Prohibition. With it came prostitution and gambling. Everyone, including the law, had turned a blind eye up until now. The vices had been good for business and, therefore, suitable for Miami Beach revenues. This was mainly because many of the area's most prominent citizens owned the brothels, imported the alcohol, and allowed gambling in their hotels.

But the fact that Al Capone had taken up residency just two doors down from Orr on Palm Island in Miami Beach was the final blow. Orr was ready to take the bull by the horns, despite his compromised health, and try to clean up the wicked little city.

"Don't say I didn't warn you, Jack," said Sam.

Jack smiled at his friend and stepped up to the podium. He looked out at the sea of faces—one hundred of the most influential men in the Miami area. Among them were prominent judges, businessmen, and politicians.

Jack cleared his throat and spoke as loudly as his compromised voice would allow.

"Miami Beach has prostituted its civic soul and raised an illegitimate progeny of lowbrow people who have become a menace to the community. It's time we returned to a God-fearing, law-abiding community or risk slipping into the welcoming hands of racketeers and the likes of Al Capone. It's time our liberal policies end. It's time to reign in illegal activities, even if that means cleaning out our own houses and the police department. I know this won't be easy. I know it's not how we've operated. I know we've been part of the problem. But it's high time we became part of the solution." Jack brought his fist down on the podium with as firm a thud as he could muster.

Applause reverberated throughout the auditorium as the men stood and affirmed their agreement in shouts and whistles. One after another, the men in the assembly took turns speaking at the podium. Some used strong language; others banged their points home with heavy fists. The meeting ended with all in agreement—they would begin a clean sweep, starting with Miami Beach, under the leadership of Jack Orr Sr.

But the plans they made were not to be. Several days later, Jack was found unconscious on the lawn in front of his home, his face bloodied and his body bruised. Dade County's Civic Digest, August 30, 1932, gave an account of what happened to him:

> *"Forced to fight barehanded against armed men for his very life, a sickly citizen of peaceful pursuits against several thugs, he may be called a martyr because that undoubtedly caused his relapse...Yet to be told is the full story of his being attacked by Capone-inspired thugs almost in front of his*

own home on Palm Island. They had to attack him there because he refused to be cowed by superior force when they demanded that he go for a ride...Mr. Orr fought with his fists against their guns and blackjacks. They downed him but were frightened off..."

No one was arrested for the assault, but it was understood Capone's henchmen wanted the man out of the way so their boss could continue his nefarious ways.

Jack Orr later died from his injuries.

~

"How horrible," said Leslie. She pulled a tissue from the box on the coffee table and dabbed her eyes.

"I agree. But of all the folks you've talked to, Orr's granddaughter seems to have the most plausible motive to possess the lockbox," said Connor.

"She lives in the panhandle," I said. "That's a long way from Deerfield Beach. Besides, how would she even know Derick Eastway let alone that he had the lockbox or what's inside?"

"Like anyone else, if she read Capone's niece's account of her uncle's life, she'd know about the money in the lockbox," said Leslie.

"Yeah, but she wouldn't know there was a key with her grandfather's name on it in the box or where the container was," I said.

"Then it's got to be someone closer to Derick Eastway. Someone who would know about the lockbox and perhaps its location," said Connor.

"But who? We've talked to the relatives of everyone we could identify on the keys. So far, no one's even hinted at the story of the lockbox or knowing Derick Eastway. So, unless the other keys we couldn't identify lead us to another relative who might have a motive, we have nowhere else to go." I forcefully closed the lid of my computer in frustration.

"What about key number nine?" asked Connor. "We don't have information on that one yet. When is Curtis expected to get back to you?"

"I'm not sure, but when he does, we can send the name to Mandy to track down the relatives. I do hope the key will provide some information we can use," I said.

"Well, Tootsie, I'm back to my newly organized house. Connor's done a magnificent job on everything," said Leslie, rising.

"I can't wait to see it, but I don't want to come by until it's all finished. Then I'll bring the champagne."

~

We didn't hear anything from Kester for a few days, then he called. I put him on speaker so both Connor and I could listen.

"So, what's the news?" asked Connor. He sat at the island counter, making a list of what he'd need to finish Leslie's project tomorrow.

"Well, you were right. Two different investigators were assigned to process the Eastway crime scenes. When I mentioned the similarity between the two crimes, they said they were looking into it. I mentioned I'd received a tip regarding an object associated with the couples' deaths. They appreciated the information but said they couldn't do anything unless you go down to Deerfield Beach station, tell them what you know, and file a report."

"I can't do that. They'll take the lockbox and keys. We need them to finish our investigation." My eyes searched Connor's for support.

"You have all the information you need to continue your search. All except the information regarding key number nine. If you surrender the lockbox, there wouldn't be any more reason you'd be in danger from the perp," Connor said.

"Except, I'd still have the information. Isn't that what he's after? The information?" Even though I didn't have the lockbox, I'd still be the target. I knew too much.

Silence filled the room.

Then Kester spoke.

"She's right, Connor. At this point, it's the information, not the keys, that the perp would want. By the way, when do you leave?"

"He leaves Sunday afternoon," I said, pushing out my lower lip at Connor.

"Connor, do you want Adele and me to stay in the cottage until you get back?" asked Kester.

"The house is secure, and I know Randi will be vigilant. But it would make me feel more comfortable for her to have someone in the guest house until we know for sure about the situation in Deerfield."

"Very well. We'll be there on Sunday before you leave. See you two then."

"I'm not helpless," I said to Connor after we hung up with Kester. "I've taken care of myself for decades. I think I can do it for a few more weeks."

"That may be, but you weren't pregnant then. It's not just your life that would be in jeopardy. The twins would be in peril, too." Connor gazed down at my growing tummy.

I let out a sigh. "You're right, of course. Thanks for reminding me I'm living for three now." I kissed Connor on the cheek.

"Isn't your appointment with the OB/GYN next week? Aren't we going to find out the gender of the twins?"

"I forgot all about it. I'll have to dangle the gender carrot when I speak to you after the visit. If you get it right, you'll get a prize."

"What kind of prize?" he asked.

"Not telling."

"Not telling, huh? I guess that means I'll have to coerce you into telling." Connor rose, winked, and gave me his seductive smile. He pulled me to him, swept my hair back, and kissed my neck.

"That won't work," I said, trying to keep my mind off his hot tender lips.

"Then, I'll have to try something more provocative." He took my hand and led me upstairs

Chapter 18

Saturday afternoon, Connor and I went to Leslie's. I couldn't wait to see her newly organized house. And, as promised, I brought champagne. I set the bottle on the dinette table in the kitchen, eager for the tour.

"Close your eyes," said Leslie. She grabbed my hand and led me through the kitchen door into the hallway. Connor followed us. "Okay, open them."

I blinked and took a step back, not believing what I saw. The hall was clear for as far as I could see. No boxes. No confining pathway.

"Oh, Leslie, it's beautifully empty!" I walked down the hall, my arms outstretched to each side. All I could feel was air—no objects impeding my walk.

"Your husband's a miracle worker," said Leslie.

"I know," I said, turning to Connor. I threw my arms around his neck and gave him a smooch. "I can't wait to see what you've done in the rooms."

Leslie opened the first door on the right and switched on the lights. My heart practically stopped when I saw shelves lining the walls from floor and ceiling and others running down the middle of the room. On the shelves were Leslie's boxes and plastic tubs, each labeled.

"And look here, Tootsie, I can reach everything without a ladder." Leslie went to a row of containers above her head and pulled on the shelf. The four-foot length ledge pulled out and eased down to her level.

"You're not only a miracle worker, but you're also a genius," I said to Connor. I gave him another big kiss. "And the other rooms? I can't wait to see them."

"Similar, except now I have several empty rooms. We'll have to figure out what to do with them."

I followed Leslie and looked into the rest of the rooms.

"I painted the rooms we put the shelves in, but the rest of the interior needs painting," said Connor. "I didn't have time to do them, too."

"We'll get Adele to help us. She'll know just what to do." I turned and applauded both of them. "Now, let's go celebrate!"

We walked to the kitchen and popped the cork on the champagne. Leslie and Connor drank a flute while I toasted their accomplishment with tea. Now Leslie could invite David to visit without any embarrassment.

~

The next afternoon, Adele and Kester moved into the cottage. We waved goodbye to Connor as he took an Uber to the airport and headed to his next assignment.

I grilled hamburgers while we sat on the patio to have dinner.

"It's so nice to have you back in the cottage, Adele. It's like old times."

When I lived in D.C., Adele moved into Boca Grande to look after the house and Bigfoot. She was going through a separation and divorce, and the arrangement worked beautifully. When I returned to Boca, she moved into the guest house, so both of us had our space. Having her close by then and again now was nice.

"Except there are three of us," she said, gazing at Kester.

"Well, don't let me cramp your style," I said with a laugh. "There's plenty of space for everybody."

"Do you want me to go to the doctor with you this week? We're dying to know what gender the babies will be," said Adele.

"That would be so nice. Almost like having Mom here." Tears filled my eyes and spilled down my cheeks. "I so wish Mom was still alive to have the excitement of knowing her grandchildren from inception."

Adele reached across the table and squeezed my hand. "My sister, your mother, is still here, and so is your father. They're inside you." Tears formed in her eyes as well.

"Of course," I said, wiping my eyes.

Little did Adele know she was only half right. While Dad was always in my heart, Mom was the only one physically inside me, thanks to Leo Barlos and his assault on her just days before her wedding.

Adele's statement brought to mind that Connor and I needed to make that appointment to see Leo as soon as Connor returned from his assignment. We'd put off this discussion far too long, and now I was showing.

On Monday, when I went to the studio, I received an email from Curtis. He said he pulled the name off key number nine and sent it to me. He also said he found something curious on the tag but couldn't see it clearly enough and thought more sophisticated equipment would better display the image. He said it wouldn't be any additional cost, but he wanted to keep the key a while. I gave him my consent.

I almost fell off my chair when I opened the Word document from Curtis and saw the name—Micah Eastway! He had to be related to Derick Eastway, but how? I immediately sent his name to Mandy. I could hardly wait for her reply to see what mystery lay behind the name.

After dinner, I sat at Leslie's dinette and turned the printed document toward her. I pointed to the name. "So, what do you think?"

She peered at the paper, then brought her hands to her cheeks. "Oh, my! This unexpected news calls for tea." Leslie rose, filled two mugs with water, and stuck them in the microwave.

"Micah has got to be related to Derick."

"Do you think Derick knew Micah's name was on the tag?" Leslie asked.

"I don't see how he could have known that. We just found out." I selected an orange spice tea bag from the bowl on the table.

"Maybe Derick always knew." Leslie looked at me through narrowed eyes.

"What do you mean?"

"What if, when he found the box, the names were legible, and Derick recognized the name?"

"Then why wouldn't he have contacted the Florida repository and looked for his name there?"

"That remains a mystery," said Leslie. "But if he didn't know to look, that means someone else knew about the name and was after the box."

My brow creased as I tilted my head. "You think Derick knew someone was after the box?"

"Exactly. And this relative may have been involved with Derick's death and came back for Sheila because he knew she had the box." Leslie returned to the table with the mugs of hot water. As we sat there in silence, pondering this possibility, we dunked our tea bags.

"But that doesn't make sense," I said. "If that person knew one of the keys had a relation's name on it, all he had to do was check with the state. He could have gotten the money at any time. Just prove he was heir to the person whose name was on the key tag. He didn't have to kill Derick or Sheila to get the money or anything else the safe deposit box held."

I wrung my tea bag and added sweetener. The hot liquid tasted good but did nothing to help us decipher this mystery.

"Maybe he was after more than his share of the money. Maybe he wanted it all, but he needed the names in the lockbox."

I sat forward; my eyes expanded. "You mean, go through the motions like we're doing to find out who these people are?" Leslie and I gazed at each other speechless. "You know what Connor would say. He'd say we're letting our imaginations run away with us, and we have no proof," I said.

"He'd be right, Tootsie." Leslie sipped her tea.

I heard from Mandy the next day. The family tree showed that Micah Eastway was Derick Eastway's father. It also showed that Derick had three children—one boy and two girls. Mrs. Eastway never mentioned her children. Both the girls lived out of state, but the son, Kyle, resided in the Tampa area, only a four-hour drive from Deerfield Beach. He was my only direct connection to the Eastways, and I wanted to interview him in person, not send a video crew. I needed to know how Micah knew Capone and what Kyle knew about the lockbox.

I looked online for the obituary of Mrs. Sheila Eastway. St. Ambrose Catholic Church in Deerfield would hold her funeral in two days. Her wake, held tomorrow evening, would be at the Babione Funeral Home in Boca Raton. I was sure both her daughters and son would be there. It was the perfect opportunity to meet her children and see if I could speak to them about Micah. I phoned David and Leslie to go with me.

We pulled up to the funeral home on Federal Highway and entered the building. The first thing we noticed was a table filled with finger foods and desserts. Next to the table was a full bar with a bartender.

"Oh, my," said Leslie. "I don't think I've ever seen alcohol served at a wake. For a somber occasion, this looks more like a celebration."

"Maybe that's the point," whispered David.

To the right was a long, narrow room with a casket set against the back wall. A large spray of red roses adorned the top. To the right on an easel was an enlargement of a photo of Sheila and Derick along with their obituaries. A couple stood in front of the easels, heads bowed, reading the information.

Back in the main foyer, dozens of people talked in groups. I asked one of the funeral personnel where Kyle and the daughters were since we'd never seen them before. The woman pointed to the three siblings, dressed in black, at various locations. Each talked to a cluster of guests.

"I'll speak with the daughter on the right," said Leslie.

"And I'll share my condolences with the daughter on the left. Randi, that leaves Kyle for you to speak with," said David.

In a way, I felt guilty being there since we didn't know the deceased except for that one encounter at my door.

But then again, we were there to ferret out a killer, if indeed there was one. If nothing else, we might be able to connect the siblings to a portion of Capone's money or whatever he had stashed in the safe deposit boxes.

Straightening my black dress, I strolled toward Kyle, letting him finish his conversations with other guests before I introduced myself. In his late forties, Derick's son appeared to be of medium height and weight with a rugged oval face, light brown hair, and blue eyes.

"My sincere condolences on the death of your mother," I said. I offered my hand in greeting. "I'm Randi Brooks. A friend of your mother's"

Kyle's pupils widened almost imperceptibly. "Thank you for coming."

"I noticed you have both your parents' pictures and obituaries in the front hall. Is the celebration of life for both of them?"

"They died so close together we thought we'd honor both, even though we already had Dad's funeral. And we wanted to do it in a way that would celebrate their lives. They enjoyed parties, so we hoped this would be a joyous occasion. A party for their parting, so to speak."

"That was a nice idea." I stood there wanting to ask him a dozen questions but had difficulty doing so at such a delicate time.

"Will you be staying in town for a while to take care of things at the house? I understand you live in the Tampa area."

"For a week or so, anyway. I'm executor of the estate." He smiled at me, but I couldn't help but feel there was something self-righteous about his statement.

"Do you mind if I come by sometime to speak with you? I've been researching a project, and the name Micah Eastway came up. I believe he was your grandfather?"

Kyle pulled back. "Why, yes, he is, but why would you be interested in him?"

"He had some connection to Al Capone. I'd love to know what that was." I handed Kyle my card. "Please call me before you leave. Our conversation could prove most beneficial to you."

Kyle cocked his head. He gave me a crooked smile and curious stare as he slipped my card into his jacket pocket. "I look forward to speaking with you." He turned to greet others offering condolences.

"Get anything from either of the sisters?" I asked as David and Leslie got into the car.

"I can tell you they're not too happy about leaving their brother here to handle the estate. Both Leslie and I got that impression," said David.

"Well, I didn't get very far with Kyle. It seemed like an awkward time to ask him about Capone and his grandfather, but he'll be in town another week or so handling the estate. I left my card and asked him to call. If I don't hear from him in a couple of days, I'll call him to set up an appointment. Mandy sent me his phone number and the Eastway address. I'm sure he'll be staying at the house."

"Please don't go alone," said David. "Kyle's the only descendent that seems to have a connection to the Eastways and lockbox. If he killed his parents for what's inside, who knows what else he'll do."

"Agreed. I'll call you when I hear from Kyle and set up an appointment."

~

On Wednesday, Adele accompanied me to the doctor's office for an ultrasound to check the babies and determine their gender. As I lay on the examining table, Cindy, the technician, squeezed the warm gel onto my abdomen and slid the transducer smoothly across my belly. She peered at the monitor as she did.

"The babies seem healthy. Strong heartbeats," she said.

"And their gender?" I asked.

"To determine the baby's gender, we look for the genitalia. See here?" Cindy pointed to the tiny image on the monitor. "This is what we call the 'hamburger effect.' A female baby's genitalia looks like a hamburger bun with a patty. Congratulations! You've got at least one little lady in there. Let's see if we can find out the gender of the other baby."

Adele squeezed my hand and grinned as Cindi continued to slide the transducer around my tummy.

"Ah-ha! The other one was hiding, but there she is. You've got twin girls, Mrs. Romero, and by the look of things, they're sharing the same placenta. That means they're identical. You can prepare the babyies' room in double pink."

Adele and I shared a warm smile as Cindy wiped the jell from my abdomen. While I dressed, she copied the ultrasound onto a CD. I would share the images with Connor when he returned.

"So, how do you feel knowing you're going to give birth to identical twin girls?" asked Adele as she drove us home.

"Honestly, the thought both excites and terrifies me. On the positive side, I remembered how wonderful growing up at Boca Grande was—playing in the sunshine, learning to swim, going to the beach, shopping for clothes. On the other hand, the reality of caring for two babies is overwhelmingly intimidating. I pray Connor and I are up to it."

"You'll have plenty of support, Randi. Between the Romeros, John and me, Adele and Todd, Archie and the company staff, you'll do just fine." She reached over in affirmation and squeezed my hand.

~

"So, how'd it go today with the ultrasound?" Connor's voice was full of anticipation.

"Hmm, okay, I guess." I leaned back against the kitchen island ankles crossed, and looked casually out the window. The pool water rippled in the breeze and sparkled in the late afternoon sunshine.

"What does that mean?" Connor's tone had turned anxious.

"It means the twins are fine."

"And?"

"And what?" I was trying to drag out the gender reveal just to tease him.

"What gender are they?"

"Guess," I said. "If you get it right, you'll get a special surprise when you get home." I wasn't sure what that would be, but I'd think of something.

"They're girls," said Connor with conviction.

I jerked upright. "How'd you know that?"

"They told me. You do know I speak to them, don't you?"

I knew Connor often laid his head against my tummy and spoke in whispers, though I never heard what he said. I guess he was already communicating with the girls.

"And I suppose they speak back?" I spoke to them every day, but I'd never heard them respond.

"Actually, they do," said Connor, his voice filled with awe.

"Well, what else did they tell you, Mr. Romero?" A smidge of jealousy crept into my tone.

"You're going to make a terrific mom."

Chapter 19

Kyle phoned me at the studio office mid-morning on Friday. I knew time was getting close to his departure, so I was thankful he called before taking off for Tampa. He said he was leaving early Sunday morning and invited me to the house on Saturday afternoon. We made an appointment for 3:00 p.m.

I phoned David to see if he was available to go with me. Unfortunately, that afternoon he volunteered at Deerfield Island Park. He said he'd try to find someone to cover for him and would call back to let me know either way. If he couldn't go, I'd have to go by myself, something I promised I wouldn't do. Yet, I couldn't let Kyle slip away without knowing what he knew.

As I sat there pondering my dilemma, I received an email from Mandy. She apologized for not sending me the additional information she'd gathered on Kyle's background and attached it to the email. He'd been married three times, was now divorced, and had two children. Both lived out of state. There was no earth-shattering information that would help the investigation, but it went to his personality. Either he made terrible decisions or couldn't keep commitments. Good thing for everyone he was now single.

I hadn't seen Archie in a long while and decided to pop into the shop. He was in his office.

"Come on in, Ms. Randi. Looks like you could use a chair." He gestured toward a wingback in front of his desk.

"Boy, could I." I dropped onto the soft cushion. Being off my feet felt good. "I know it's been a while, but you wanted to talk to me about something. It's been so hectic I haven't had a chance to sit down and have an extended conversation with you. What did you want to talk to me about?"

Archie fidgeted in his chair. "I'm not sure even how to start. This has to do with a call I got through the ministry from a Pauline Kincade."

"I'm sure you gave her the benefit of your wisdom. I doubt I could add anything to your advice." From the number of comments Archie was getting to his online show, Living Without Regret, he fulfilled a need in many hearts.

"She started out looking for spiritual advice, Miss Randi, but it morphed into something else altogether. She was looking for closure on a crime she said occurred in two thousand."

"Two thousand? That was a long time ago. Surely, she checked out all the reports online, at the courts, or other resources."

"Said she did, but she believes there was a cover-up. She wants someone to find out what really happened. Who were the people involved. That's why I wanted to speak with you. I think this is an investigation you and Connor should get involved with."

"Us? Why?"

"The police ruled the death a suicide, but she says it was murder. She wants the case reopened, but she needs her theories corroborated by professionals so the file can be taken to the Florida Department of Law Enforcement."

I sat back. Pauline's situation was definitely out of my wheelhouse.

"I sympathize with Pauline. I do, Archie, but I don't think we can add anything to our schedule with the business and the babies coming. Besides, right now, we're trying to solve another old mystery. I'll need to speak with Connor.."

"I understand. But she's very passionate about this and says she has proof that the police botched the investigation. Just give her a call, Miss Randi. The least you can do is speak to her before saying 'no.'" Archie's dark eyes pleaded for a positive response as he handed me her contact information.

"I'll talk to Connor, but no promises," I said, holding up my palms.

Just as I walked out of Archie's office, David called.

"Hey, David. So, you're choosing gopher tortoises over our investigation?" I scolded.

"You know I'd be there if I could. I'm still working on finding a substitute, but no one's available so far. I'll keep trying."

"Thanks. I don't want to go there without you, but Kyle's leaving Sunday morning. If I miss him tomorrow, I'll have to travel to Tampa to see him. I want to avoid that if I can."

"I should hope so, especially after what I've found out."

A tingle of adrenalin rushed through me. "What do you mean?"

"I did some more digging into Kyle's background. He's quite the shady character. No wonder his sisters were concerned about him being the executor of the estate."

I gulped. "What did you find out?"

"Don't ask me how I obtained this information, but suffice it to say, it comes from trustworthy sources."

"You're scaring me, David."

"I don't mean to scare you, just to let you know the kind of man you're dealing with. The bottom line, Randi, is that Kyle's an accomplished computer hacker and identity thief. He got into computers as a young man when they were just coming out in the 1980s. He worked as a computer center manager for Radio Shack and left the company in his late twenties. He formed his own computer consulting company, sold it five years later, then realized he could make even more money through selling hacked information to the highest bidder. He's been on the FBI's radar for years. Of course, they haven't been able to catch him yet, but his signature seems to be on dozens of crimes. He's very clever and leaves few bread crumbs in his wake."

"Interesting information, but how do his computer hacking and identity theft relate to our investigation?"

"After I found out about his computer hacking career, on a whim, I went back through the Florida Department of Financial Services, Division of Unclaimed Property. Guess what I found?"

"David, quit keeping me in suspense!" Couldn't he just tell me without all the drama?

"Three names from the list I checked on before no longer have anything in the repository. Nada. Nothing. Either the rightful owners took out the goods, or someone else did."

"What?" I yelled into the phone. "How'd they get whatever it was out of the repository? I never told any of my interviewees about the unclaimed property department or anything about what might be there."

"Well, it seems uncanny that just as we're looking into this, relatives of three of the people whose names were on the tags requested what was in their box."

"What were the names of those no longer on the list?" I needed to call those I'd interviewed to find out if they had contacted the division.

"Robert Hanley, Ilsa Carpuchi, and Lena Gallucci," said David.

"I can call two of their relatives right now, but the account of Lena's relationship with Capone was through a taped interview. I never spoke to her relatives, so I wouldn't know about her. I'll get back to you after I speak to Sue Cameron and Ray Hanley." I hung up without saying goodbye.

My finger shook as I tapped my way to Sue's phone number.

"Oh, hello, Randi. I hope your week is going well. How's your investigation coming?" Sue's voice was just as I remembered—perky—but I could also hear the cadence in her voice.

"Just fine." I tried to make my voice as normal as possible, but I wasn't sure I was doing a very good job.

"Do you need more information?" Sue asked.

"Just a couple of follow-up questions, if you have the time."

"Sure. I'm at the fitness center on the treadmill. I've got another twenty minutes of walking."

I swallowed hard. "Have you made any calls lately to the Florida Department of Financial Services, Division of Unclaimed Property?"

"The what? I've never heard of them. Why do you ask?" Her voice was calm but curious. I could hear her deep breaths.

"I think someone may have removed something from their repository that rightfully belonged to your grandmother. Since you're a granddaughter, the item might belong to you."

"What is it?"

"Unfortunately, I don't know. I was hoping you had claimed it and could tell me."

"Sorry. I don't know anything about it."

"Do you happen to have a security system monitoring your personal information such as your driver's license, credit cards, Social Security number, things like that?" I paced the office, trying to think of the ways someone could have assumed her identity.

The claiming of an item from the state repository was processed electronically. If someone wanted to, what stopped them from using one of the names on the key tags, impersonating a relative, fraudulently reproducing the necessary documents, and retrieving whatever the safe deposit box held? Yeah, that would take time and skill. But it didn't seem too difficult for someone experienced in hacking and identity theft.

"I don't. Too expensive on a limited income. Do you think I've been the victim of identity theft?" Sue's voice carried an edge of panic, and her breathing seemed faster.

"I don't know, but it wouldn't hurt to check. Has anything unusual happened lately, such as someone hacking into your Facebook, email account, or your computer?"

There was silence.

"Now that you mention it, something strange did happen about a week ago. I got an email from my bank confirming I had changed the password to my online account and transferred one thousand dollars from my savings account through Xchange. This system allows bank customers to transfer money to another through their email or cell phone number. I don't even use XChange. When I contacted the bank, they said someone had fraudulently accessed my online banking through XChange and transferred the money to someone else's account. The bank locked my accounts, and I had to open new accounts and change my password. Do you think these incidents are related to the questions you're asking?" asked Sue.

"They could be," I said. "I'm not a cyber security expert, but it does seem curious these two things happened around the same time. I may have more information for you soon. In the meantime, please have someone check to make sure your identity is secure."

"I'll do it right away, and thanks for calling."

"I'm sorry to have alarmed you, Sue, but in this day and age, no one is safe from cybercriminals."

"Isn't that the truth."

My next call went to Frank Hanley. He said he hadn't contacted the Florida Department of Financial Services, Division of Unclaimed Property either, but had a similar experience as Sue regarding XChange and his baking account. These two incidents seemed too similar to be a coincidence. If both Frank and Sue, whose relative's names were on one of Capone's keys, had their emails compromised and something stolen from the state repository, it made perfect sense to me who the culprit was—Kyle Eastway.

I phoned David and told him what I'd found. He wasn't surprised and assumed the same perpetrator committed the crimes.

"Randi, I'm sorry I can't go with you tomorrow. I haven't been able to find anyone to cover for me at the park, and reservations are full. Please assure me you're not going over to Kyle's alone," said David.

"I'll think of something. We've got to know what he took, how he did it, and why."

"And you think he's going to tell you?"

"I'll pry it out of him if necessary," I said with a laugh.

I phoned Connor to discuss my meeting with Kyle.

"I'm dead set about you not going to his home, honey. You don't know anything about this man, except what Mandy and David told you, and that's not so positive. Even though we don't know for sure he's involved with any of this, you need to be cautious. I'm not telling you not to see him to gather information about his grandfather, just to hold your meeting in a public place where there are plenty of people."

"Like Two Georges?" The restaurant was public and directly across the Intracoastal from the Eastways' home.

"Perfect. And don't veer from this topic. You'll strike close to home if you ask too many questions and may tip your hand. Also, I'll phone Kester and ask him to pose as a customer and sit close by, so he can keep an eye on you. Only then will I feel comfortable about your meeting with Kyle."

After hearing back from Connor that Kester would attend the rendezvous, I phoned Kyle. He agreed to the change of venue.

~

When I arrived at Two Georges, I found Kyle sitting at the long wooden bar drinking a beer. I grabbed a stool beside him. I knew the restaurant well but usually sat in the outdoor seating area.

"Quite the display," I said, pointing to the wall behind the bar.

Over the wall-sized mirror dangled a brown fishing net decorated with shells, starfish, spiny urchins, and skeletons of other sea creatures. In the center hung a huge sailfish. Its blue and gray coloration, impressive dark blue dorsal fin, and long bill made a striking decoration. How sad to think the fish's beautiful life ended only to allow us to ogle at its remains. I was thankful many of today's fishermen chose to catch and release game fish instead of taking trophies.

"You do know they don't catch sailfish with a net, don't you? A heavy-duty rod and reel would have been more realistic." Kyle took a swig of his beer. Instead of looking at me, he eyed my reflection in the mirror

"But the display wouldn't have been as attractive," I said. As I gazed into the mirror, I caught Kester's reflection. He was seated in a booth opposite the bar. I nodded slightly.

"Ginger ale," I said as the bartender approached.

"What, nothing stronger?" asked Kyle. "It's almost Saturday night. Time to relax."

"That may be, but my girls don't care what day or time it is, only that they remain comfortable."

The bartender put down a napkin and set my drink on it.

"Your girls?" asked Kyle.

I looked down at my noticeable swelling tummy and rubbed my hands over it.

"I see," said Kyle. "That complicates things." His stern eyes darted around the bar as though searching for a piece to a puzzle.

"Complicates things?"

"Sure. You'll go from two to four in no time at all. Are you prepared for that?" He looked at me curiously.

"I...I think so." That seemed an odd question, coming from a hacker and possibly a cold-blooded killer.

"So, what did you want to see me about?" Kyle gulped what remained of his beer, signaled the bartender, and ordered another.

"While doing some research about Deerfield Island Park, I came upon some names associated with Al Capone back in the 1930s. Since you live just down from the park, I'm sure your father told you the story about Capone's little fish business on the Intracoastal and his subsequent purchase of what is now the park." I turned slightly toward Kyle, rested my elbow on the bar, and chin on my fist.

"Can't live in Deerfield for any length of time and not know about Capone and the island," Kyle said, his gaze never wavering from the mirror.

"Well, as I mentioned at the funeral, one of those names was Micah Eastway, your grandfather. I was hoping you could tell me how he met Capone and his relationship with the Chicago kingpin. I hope you don't mind if I record what you say." I pulled a digital recorder from my bag, placed it on the bar, and switched it on. The green light indicated it was recording.

Kyle looked down at the device, then at me. "Sure," he said with a growl.

"Anytime you're ready."

~

Deerfield Beach 1927

Micah saw the car before it was even within earshot of the garage. From his vantage point high in the arms of the oak tree, he could see a long way north down Dixie Highway, almost into Palm Beach, the next county. As the black sedan rambled closer, the young boy scrambled from the limb, dropped to the ground, and ran to the front of the garage.

He wanted to get to the roadside before the automobile got there so he could stand in front of Eastway's Garage, the only one for miles, and wave at the people as they drove by. It was one of his favorite pastimes—watching the people whiz by, wondering where they came from and where they were going. One of these days, when he was older, he'd be in a car going somewhere. The year was 1928, the height of Prohibition. Micah was twelve.

As the car drew nearer, it slowed. Then it pulled off the highway onto the coral rock driveway in front of the garage. Micah's heart pounded as the tires crunched over the crushed coral. He'd never seen such a fancy car before. Dust covered it, of course, but it would sparkle like a new pocket watch with a bit of soap and water. The driver's door opened, and a large man got out. Sweat stained his shirt from the hot, muggy, South Florida summer air.

"Can I help you, mister?" Micah squinted in the noonday sun as he pulled the drooped strap from his overalls up over his shoulder, smoothed out his hair as best he could, and walked toward the man.

"Your father here?" asked the driver.

"No, sir. He's out on the farm, but I can help you. You need some gas, oil, your windows cleaned?" As Micah walked closer to the car, he noticed a man seated in the back seat.

"I've got a low tire. I think it's got a leak."

Micah walked around the car and inspected the tires. "That right front tire looks mighty low. That the one giving you trouble? Better not travel too much farther on it. If it goes completely flat, you'll damage the rim. Then you'll have a big problem. The next garage is five miles down the highway." Micah gestured toward the road as he stood in his bare feet, looking up at the man who towered above him like a stone wall.

"Hey, kid. You're pretty smart," said the driver.
"I've worked here with my dad since I was five. I know pretty much everything there is to know about a car. You want me to change your tire?"
"You're just a young whippersnapper. How are you gonna change a tire?" asked the driver, who looked down at Micah, hands on his hips.
"I may be young, but I know how to change a tire and fix a flat. Just wait and see."
The man hesitated, then acquiesced. "Go ahead and change the tire. Then check the old one. If it's got a leak, fix it."
"Your passenger will have to get out," said Micah. "We have a waiting room inside the office with cold pop—orange, grape, cola, and rootbeer. Maybe you'd like to wait in there." He flicked his head in the direction of the open door.
The man didn't move.
"You and your passenger will need to wait inside, and I'll need the car keys." Micah held out his palm. The driver reluctantly tossed Micah the keys. He caught them as adeptly as catching a fly ball, something he'd done for years on the makeshift diamond in the sandlot behind the garage.
The driver opened the car's back door, poked his head in, and spoke to the passenger. A few seconds later, another man exited the vehicle. His round face didn't seem familiar to Micah, but the scars on his cheek did. Where had he seen them before? A newspaper or magazine article his parents showed him? He couldn't remember.
"Come on, boss. We can wait in there." The driver motioned toward the open door of the office. Both men went inside.
Micah climbed into the driver's seat. His eyes bulged as he inspected the car's interior. He'd never seen

anything like it—black leather, polished wood, shining brass. He adjusted the driver's seat for his shorter legs, inserted the key into the ignition, and drove the car into the garage. There he set to work jacking up the car, removing the tire, and replacing it with the spare. Then, he pulled out the leaky innertube.

He placed the tube in a tub of water and pressed it down until he saw air bubbles sprinting out of a pin-sized hole, indicating the leak's location. Marking an X on the spot with a white grease pencil, he removed the inner tube from the tub and dried it off. After roughing up the rubber around the leak, he placed glue about the hole and stuck a black rubber patch on it. The glue dried in fifteen minutes. Micah then fitted the tube back into the tire, filled it with air, and placed the tire back into the car's trunk to be used as the spare. The whole process took him about forty minutes.

Micah poked his head into the office. "Mister, your car's ready. That'll be a dollar fifty." He wiped his hands on a grease-smeared towel.

The men looked at Micah in amazement. They walked out to the car and circled it, paying particular attention to the right front tire.

"You did a good job, kid. We're lucky you were here. What's your name?" asked the man with the scars.

"Micah. Micah Eastway."

The man pulled out a ten-dollar bill from his wallet and handed it to Micah.

The boy's eyes widened to see such a large bill. "I'm sorry, sir, but we don't have change." Micah returned the bill to the man.

"That's okay, son. You keep the change for your tip."

Micah looked down at the ten spot. *"Thanks, mister!"* He could hardly contain his smile. His father would never believe this. *"Thanks a bunch."* He extended his hand toward the man. The man's sizeable meaty hand engulfed Micah's small but strong one as they shook.

"We'd best be going, boss," said the driver.

"Sure," said the man.

"Where are you from, and where are you headed?" asked Micah.

"From Chicago. Headed to Miami Beach," said the man.

"I hear Miami's a nice place. Have a safe trip." Micah watched as the men got into the car. He waved to them as they pulled out onto the highway. The man in the back seat waved back. Micha's gaze followed the sedan until it crossed the railroad tracks and drove out of sight.

Chapter 20

"So, your grandfather met Al Capone?" I asked.

"Of course, he didn't know it was the notorious gangster at the time. It wasn't until several months later, when he noticed a photo of the man with the scar in a copy of the *Miami Daily News*, that he realized who he was."

"It's funny how Capone seemed to be such a dichotomy of a man. I've found him at times overly generous, and at other times, overly evil." I clicked off the recorder.

"Isn't that like most of us? Charming on the outside, secrets on the inside? Even you, Ms. Brooks. I'm sure there are reasons why you're asking questions about my grandfather that you're not telling me."

A shiver ran through me. "I don't have a clue what you're talking about."

"Don't play coy with me," Kyle said in a low, gruff voice. "You know much more than you're letting on."

Time to go.

"It was nice speaking with you, Kyle, and I appreciate the story about your grandfather, but I've got to run." I gathered my bag and recorder, signaled the bartender for my tab, and slid off the stool.

Kyle waited for me to pay my bill, then tossed a twenty onto the bar and got up as well. He followed me toward the restaurant's exit.

Panic gripped me. Knowing a potential killer was steps behind me, I took a quick right close to the exit and rushed to the ladies' room. I went into a stall, locked the door, and slumped against it. My heart pounded in my throat; my breathing came in gasps. Kester had always been there when I needed him. Where was he now?

A full ten minutes passed before I calmed down. I was sure Kyle had left and was already home by that time. I gingerly opened the door and peeked out—no sign of him. Crossing back toward the bar to where Kester had been seated, I scanned the booth for him. Empty. Figuring he saw me leave, he must have gone as well.

I jumped when my phone rang. Kester.

"Randi, where are you? I saw you leave with Kyle behind you and followed him out of the restaurant. I watched him get into his car and pull out but didn't see you in the parking lot. I figured you'd left as well. I'm almost at Boca Grande."

"I'm still at the restaurant," I said as I weaved through the tables toward the exit. "I took a little detour and went to the restroom to ditch Kyle. I'm just leaving now."

"I'll park in front of the house and wait until I see you drive in."

"Should be there in a few minutes." I punched off the phone and stashed it in my bag.

Dusk settled in as I left the restaurant. Scanning the parking lot before walking to my car, I was relieved Kyle wasn't anywhere in sight. Just the usual heavy Saturday evening crowd, their cars crammed like sardines in the parking lot. When I got to my Passat, I pressed the remote, opened the door, and tossed my bag onto the passenger's seat.

"Don't scream. Don't make a sound, or it'll be your last."

I stiffened at the familiar male voice and the rigid object pressed against my back, emphasizing his threat. Kyle had come up behind me, hemming me in between two cars. My mind raced as I scanned my surroundings. Was there an escape route? None that I could see.

"Let's take a walk," he said.

He backed up, pulling me with him until we were free of the cars. I almost tripped as he shoved me forward with the point of what I presumed was the barrel of a handgun. If I'd had only myself to think of, I might have screamed or made a run for it. But I had the babies to think of; I couldn't do anything foolish.

"Where are we going?" I asked, trying to keep my cool. All the while, a sinking feeling worked its way through me.

"Not far. Just walk." Kyle moved beside me and entwined his arm tightly in mine as though we were lovers out for a stroll.

His hand and gun rested in the pocket of his jacket as he guided me toward Hillsborough Boulevard and across the J.D. Butler Bridge at the Intracoastal. Had this been any other time, it would have been a perfect evening for a romantic walk—a gentle breeze, the moon rising over the beach, the glow of lights reflecting off the swift incoming tide. The only things breaking the serenity of the night were the whine of tires over the draw-bridge and my circumstances.

"Don't do this, Kyle," I pleaded as we crossed the apex of the bridge.

"Can't stop now. You know too much." His heavy footsteps reverberated on the steel grating of the bridge.

"Not really. All I have are interviews from relatives of people who encountered Capone."

"Yeah, but you wouldn't have that if you didn't have the lockbox. See what I mean about keeping secrets?" Kyle's voice turned hard, menacing. His grip tightened on my arm.

"How'd you know I had it?"

"I'd heard the story of the lockbox from my father ever since I was a child. I'd even seen the names on the tags, written them down. It wasn't until recently that I thought more seriously about the opportunity attached to the keys. I asked my father to give me the lockbox, but he'd already heard about who the FBI suspected I was. After that, I knew I'd never get my hands on the box. Dad and I struggled."

"And you hit him over the head."

"Yes, but he died of a heart attack," Kyle corrected. "I do regret that." His voice reflected the only semblance of empathy I'd seen thus far.

"Why'd you do it? You didn't need the money from the safe deposit boxes. From what I understand, you've got plenty, or at least have ways of getting plenty."

"How naive you are. In my line of work, it's not only the money, it's the challenge of the game. Doing something that's never been done before. Seeing how good you are. Pushing yourself to the limit, to be the best." He lifted his head, smiled, and gazed toward the beach as though having received some accolade for his nefarious plan.

"Only you didn't have the lockbox."

"It was evidence of what I was doing. I needed to destroy it."

"But your father gave the box to your mother. And she gave it to me."

"I didn't know where it was, though I looked thoroughly through the house. It wasn't until my mother's funeral, when you mentioned my grandfather and Capone, that it dawned on me you knew about the lockbox. The only deduction I could make is that she'd given it to you. After I looked up who you were, it made sense."

Kyle steered me right at SE 19th Avenue and again at SE 1st Street on the other side of the bridge. On SE 18th Avenue, he led me south several blooks to a home that sat on a large lot right on the Intracoastal. There weren't any lights on.

"This your house?" I hoped there'd be some neighbors out in the yards, someone I could signal—no such luck.

"Yeah, now that my parents are gone." Kyle opened the door and shoved me through it.

In the waning light, I stumbled but managed to catch myself on the arms of a chair in the foyer before I went sprawling onto the slate floor.

"Did you kill her? Your mother?"

"Alcohol and pills make a deadly mix. She'd drank for years. It was simply a matter of time before she mixed up her pills in a stupor."

"With a little help from you, I'll wager. And then you ransacked the house, looking for the lockbox."

Kyle grabbed my arm and pulled me to a standing position. "Move over there and sit down." Kyle removed the gun from his pocket and gestured toward a contemporary side chair.

I moved in its direction, taking in my surroundings—a sizeable, well-furnished, terra cotta tiled living room surrounded by sliding glass doors that looked out onto the Intracoastal. At the seawall were a long dock and a tethered boat with outboards. I sat.

"You've thrown a monkey wrench into my plans. I spent hours, days, weeks with this plan. I was so close, but you had to interfere. Now, I've got to figure out what to do with you." Kyle paced the room and drew his hand through his dark hair, all the while keeping his eyes and weapon pointed at me. Beads of sweat dotted his upper lip.

What is he planning?

"I'm curious. What was in the state repository under Micah's name?"

"Ha!" spit Kyle, his eyes growing wide. "You think I'd tell you? Suffice it to say, what was inside was well worth my time." He stared at me with frigid eyes. I could see him formulating the skeleton of a sinister plot behind them.

"Worth the probability of spending the rest of your life in jail and dying there?" I didn't know if he feared death, but dying in jail alone didn't seem like a pleasant way to go.

"They haven't caught me yet, and I don't intend for them to."

"I'm sure it's just a matter of time before the police figure out the connection between your parents, the lockbox, and grand theft using your skills as a hacker and identity thief. Fact is, they already know about it. I'm sure they'll be here any moment." I stretched the truth but hoped Kester wasn't far behind when I didn't show at Boca Grande.

"By the time someone gets here, I'll be long gone, and so will you. Let's go." Kyle yanked me from the chair and pushed me toward one of the sliding doors. "Open it," he commanded.

I flicked up the lock and pulled the handle. The large glass door slid open seamlessly. Kyle nudged me down the sidewalk and onto the dock with the gun in my back. Almost dark, lights from the J.D. Butler Bridge, The Cove shopping center, and Two Georges across the waterway flickered off the rolling incoming tide as the water charged speedily north toward the bridge

"Get in." Kyle gestured toward the boat.

"We going for a ride?" I slowly moved toward it.

"I'm going for a ride. You're going along for shark bait."

I stopped dead in my tracks. "Shark bait! You're taking me out to sea so you can toss me overboard for shark bait?" Connor! The babies! Tears streamed down my cheeks.

"Get into the boat!" he yelled, digging the gun into my ribs.

There must be a way out. Think!

I stumbled toward the boat. Then, taking two quick steps in recovery, I left my sandals behind and dove off the end of the dock into the rushing black waters of the Intracoastal. As I surfaced in the dark, cool liquid, the fast incoming tide snatched me, flinging me toward the bridge. I heard the crack of Kyle's gun. Then, a bullet whizzed by me. I dove under the obsidian water.

If I swam diagonally to the current, I'd eventually make it across the Intracoastal and away from Kyle. I might even make my way past the bridge to Sullivan Park. Coral rocks bordered the park at the shoreline that could cut my feet, but at least I'd be alive. Past the park, the next stop would be Capone Island. After that, the tide would pull me toward Boca and the inlet. Who knew where I'd end up? Maybe as shark bait, after all.

I swam underwater until my lungs screamed for air. When I surfaced gasping, I could see I'd made some headway yet was unprepared for the current's strength. Terror surged through me as the rapid tide tossed me off-angle and swept me toward the bridge where the water narrowed. If I couldn't control my angle or speed, I'd hit the bridge pilings, breaking whatever part of my body came in contact with the concrete structure. I kicked and stroked as though my life depended upon it.

It did.

Scared and cold, but with adrenaline pumping through me, the thought I needed to make it to shore for the girls' sake kept me moving forward. Fortunately, I missed the pilings as I passed under the bridge. I was so close to Sullivan Park I could practically feel the land, but the current pushed me past it to where the Hillsboro Canal and Intracoastal met. There, the water and current split. The main flow continued north up the Intracoastal toward Boca; the other swept west. Between the two currents just in front of Capone Island was an eddy. Unsure whether the water should go north or west, the current became entangled in a confusing pool of dangerous rotating water. This was where I landed.

The water whirled me around and around. With every kick and stroke, the circling liquid forced me back into its vortex. My head spun, and after several minutes of fighting the pull of the swirling water, my strength gave out, my legs and arms useless. I finally gave up and flopped over, desperate for air. Making myself as large as possible—legs and arms outstretched—I tried to slow my rotation.

Gulping for breath, the first twinkling stars in the darkening sky rotated above me. I closed my eyes and prayed for a means of escape. The sound of the lapping water echoed in my ears and spilled across my face. Brackish water filled my nostrils and nasal cavities with its stinging liquid, then found my throat, choking me.

With my life and that of the girls hanging in the balance, I dug deep into my long-forgotten water survival skills training. Expending the last of my strength, I inhaled and dove down into the eddy. About eight feet under, the rotating water released me, and I found the sandy bottom of the canal. Pushing off, I angled away from the spinning liquid. When I surfaced, miraculously, I was headed toward the island.

Barely making out a small beach, I paddled toward the shore and dragged my drained body onto the sand. I lay there, lungs heaving and my body shivering uncontrollably from cold and sheer exhaustion. The sound of my heart pounded in my ears, yet I thanked God I was alive and had made it away from Kyle and onto land.

It seemed hours before my heart returned to normal. I struggled to stand, but my arms and legs were spent. Letting out a grunt, I collapsed face down into the sand. Tears gushed from my eyes.

"Randi?"

I lifted my head with great difficulty to find David standing over me, flooding the area with light from a lantern. He knelt beside me, turned me over, and wrapped his arms around my trembling, sand-encrusted body.

"What happened?" he asked. "Was it Kyle?" He gently brushed the sand from my cheek.

I nodded. "How did you find me?" I asked, my weak voice hoarse from swallowing the briny water.

"A guest lost her cell phone along the path, so I came back to look for it. That's when I saw you. I'm calling Kester. He called me a little while ago and said you never came home after being with Kyle. He tried your cell, but you never picked up. He was on his way to the Eastway house." David punched in Kester's number and spoke to him briefly. "He's going to meet us at the dock at Sullivan Park."

David helped me to my feet and supported my wobbly legs as he guided me along the path. When we reached the welcome center, he found a towel in lost and found and draped it around my shivering shoulders.

"You were right. Kyle stole the contents of the three safe deposit boxes, and he was planning to steal what was inside the rest of them. That was bad enough, but the worst thing is, he was about to take me out into the ocean on his boat, dump me overboard, and feed me to the sharks!" The words and horror at the thought caught in my throat. The possibility that I'd have lost not only my life but that of the twins hit me big time. I wept uncontrollably and leaned into David as he held my lurching shoulders.

Kester met us with a paramedic unit at the dock at Sullivan Park. After being transported to the emergency room of Boca Raton Regional Hospital and checked out thoroughly by the doctor, he drove me home. Adele met me at the door. She enveloped me in her arms and held me tight as I sobbed.

"The doctor says she and the babies are fine. She just needs a hot bath, some food, and a good night's sleep," said Kester.

"Come on, honey, let me help you upstairs," said Adele. "I'll run you a hot bath. John, please make Randi some hot tea and something to eat."

My legs quivered as my aunt helped me climb the stairs.

Adele and Kester stayed in the house that night. After Connor rushed home the next day, they moved back to

Adele's. It took me a few days to recover physically, but the emotional scars of almost losing my life and that of the twins would take time.

Connor hadn't said a word about the incident since he got home. Of course, he showered me with hugs and kisses when he first saw me, but I couldn't tell if he was suppressing his anger or simply thankful the babies and I made it out of that harrowing experience in one piece. We sat at the island eating salads.

"Don't you think it's time we talked about it? I know you're angry with me, but I did everything you said: a public place, Kester watching, leaving when things felt uncomfortable." I pushed a carrot around my plate.

"I know, Randi, but the thought of losing you and the girls overwhelmed me with emotions I've never experienced." Connor turned and cupped my face in his hands. Tears trickled from the corners of his eyes. "How could I go on without you?" He inhaled and began to sob, the pent-up tension vibrating his shoulders with every breath.

I stood and pulled him to me, holding him until we shed our last tear. We'd never been so emotionally close.

~

I returned to the studio several days later to continue my work. While in the control room, Rachel popped in. We'd talked on the phone during the last few days, but this was the first time we'd seen each other.

"Randi. I can't imagine what you've been through." She hugged me tightly.

I pulled back and smiled. "Yeah. Who would have thought my high school swimming and water safety training would come in so handy?"

"Well, I hope that's your last caper. You can't afford to get involved in another one, especially now." Rachel sat.

"You're right. At least, not until after the twins arrive." My life-threatening experience with Kyle made me realize I wouldn't be up to another caper for a long time.

"And then?"

I shrugged and fingered a paper clip. "I don't know. Maybe nothing, maybe something a bit more benign." I hoped I didn't have to give up my capers altogether. I did enjoy them.

"I'm sure you heard the Broward County Marine Patrol picked up Kyle just inside the Hillsboro Inlet as he was heading out to sea."

"Kester told us. I'm so glad. No telling what kind of damage that man has and could have done. At least now he'll be put away, and the rest of the people whose names were on Capone's key tags can get what belongs to them."

"Any idea what was inside the safe deposit boxes?"

"Kyle never said. Only that it was worth his while."

"I don't want to thrust you into something you're not ready for, but what about moving ahead with our live stream project? Have you and Connor discussed it?" Rachel gazed at me with hopeful eyes.

"We have talked about it."

Rachel grabbed my hands. "And?"

"And, we want to move forward with it. We think it will be a great boost to the studio and the business, not to mention increasing awareness for greyhound adoption. We hope to raise enough money to make significant donations to other charities as well, including Archie's ministry."

Rachel jumped up. So did I.

"Whoo-hoo!" we said in unison, embracing and jumping around the control booth as though we were still in high school putting on the talent show. Our jubilation brought back memories.

"Well, no time to waste, then," said Rachel. "I did some preliminary research before, but now I can move ahead and try to pin down some companies to help us, find sponsors, put a budget together. We only have a few months to pull this off before you give birth, so I'll be putting pedal to the metal to make it happen. Gotta run, Randi. Talk later." Rachel hugged me, then rushed out of the room and back to her office, leaving me in the wake of her whirlwind.

I had a lot to do myself in preparation for the actual show, including editing the video interviews we completed and planning voiceovers of the recorded stories. Plus, I wanted to arrange for someone to go back to Thelma's and interview her on camera. And I needed to call Reverend Lester Pearson to tell him about the safe deposit box and see if he would consent to being part of the show. If not, we could work around it, but having a pastor open a safe deposit box on camera to reveal what Al Capone hid inside under his father's name would add a great deal of credibility to the event. All this in just over three months.

Chapter 21

Over the next three months, the studio was awhirl with organizational meetings involving outside vendors who would be part of Capone's Keys' grand production. Our other in-studio productions came to a standstill while Rachel, with our help, orchestrated all the logistics. This included program design to online viewer ticket sales and live streaming specialists, local and national sponsorships to coveted in-studio seating, merchandise design and sales to media coordination and security.

I didn't' think Rachel slept a wink or saw her kids during that time. The financial future of the studio, our programs, and the support of the nonprofit hung on the success of this production, and she vowed to make sure there were no glitches. Besides, all this was her idea. Pulling it off would be the crowning achievement of her career and that of A Stitch In Time. Everything had to go perfectly.

"Hey, how about some coffee?" I waddled into Rachel's office around 10:00 a.m. carrying two large cups, one filled with her favorite java—sugar cookie almond milk latte.

"You're a lifesaver," she said, stretching her hand across the desk to grab the cup as though she'd expire if she didn't have a gulp.

"I don't know how you do it. I knew you were good, but what you've done with this production is over the top, and beyond anything we could have dreamed of." I sat on the edge of a chair, the only few inches of space in the office not covered by something to do with the production.

Rachel pointed to the opened three-ring binder in front of her, bursting with tabs and pages. "If it weren't for this, I'd be sunk. The sacred book of Capone's Keys, every book, every chapter, every verse." She wiggled her perfectly penciled eyebrows at me, only one of her facial features flawlessly made up. How she managed to look so beautiful all the time, even under duress, was a marvel. But then, she'd been that way ever since our high school days.

"Only a week away. Are you excited?" I sipped my caffeine-free tea.

"That's not the word for it. But look at you. Do you think the twins will wait until after the production? You look like you could deliver any time. Now that's excitement."

"I wouldn't miss our live streaming of Capone's Keys for anything in the world. Except for giving birth to twins, I mean." I looked at Rachel and shrugged.

"You do know they could come at any second." She gazed at me with concern.

"I do. Well, I'll leave you with your sacred book. Connor and I have an appointment." I got up to leave.

"With someone interesting, I hope."

I blew Rachel a kiss. "Give us a call if you need anything."

"You're last on my list, considering your condition." Rachel let out a soft laugh.

As I left Rachel's office, I wasn't looking forward to our appointment. While Connor and I were finally ready to sit down and discuss the future of our relationship and that of the twins with Leo Barlos, it would be an uncomfortable conversation. Why we waited so long, I'll never know, not that now was ideal either, but at least we'd get things settled before the babies arrived. That should allow some peace of mind.

"Everything alright with Rachel?" asked Connor. He had waited in the car while I visited with her.

"Everything's fine. She's one organized and amazing person. How she pulls everything together with what seems like so little effort blows me away. But then, she's always been like that. Thank heaven I snatched her from the Historical Society when the studio was just a seed of an idea. We wouldn't be where we are today if it weren't for her. She secured our first sponsor—Leo."

"Does she know about him?" Connor briefly looked at me.

"I never told her." I rested my hands on my bulging tummy.

"How do you think she'll react if our discussion goes south and the studio loses its primary sponsor, especially right before Capone's Keys?"

"She won't be happy, of course, but once she knows the reason why, she'll understand. Our relationship is far more valuable than sponsorship money."

Connor pulled into the parking lot outside Leo's commercial real estate office. He gazed at me before getting out. "Well, we're here. Are you ready?"

"As I'll ever be," I said, though now that I was here, I wasn't so sure.

I'd been in Leo's office several times over the past couple of years, always under unpleasant circumstances. First, there was a fire at the upholstery shop—one I knew he was involved in but could never prove. The blaze had destroyed Archie's office and required us to rent warehouse space from Leo to keep the upholstery business alive until the construction company finished the necessary repairs.

The second time was confronting him regarding the assault on my mother, forcing him to acknowledge his despicable behavior and that he was my biological father. That had led him to generously gift me the property next to A Stitch in Time to ease his conscience. And that led to my building the studio. A positive outcome, I supposed, but I'd have traded it all for a different scenario altogether. Now, here I was again, trying to turn something negative into something positive. Would dredging up the past with him in it ever end?

"Good morning, Mr. and Mrs. Romero. Mr. Barlos is expecting you." Carrie Lee, Leo's administrative assistant, rose from her desk and escorted us to his office. "May I get you anything? Coffee? Tea? Water?"

"Water would be nice," I said. My mouth seemed inordinately dry.

Carrie opened Leo's office door and gestured toward two chairs across from his desk.

"Please have a seat. I'll be right back with your water. Mr. Barlos should be here any minute; he's running a bit late."

Connor and I sat, staring at Leo's empty chair. I guess he wasn't expecting us after all. A moment later, Carrie popped in with our water. Suddenly, a side door burst open, and in strode Leo's robust form, carrying two large gifts in colorful baby wrapping paper.

"So sorry I'm late. I thought I'd get here before you arrived. These are for you." Leo handed Connor and me each a gift. "For the babies," he said, smiling.

I looked at the package, then at him.

"That wasn't necessary." I didn't know what else to say.

"Don't be silly. You'll be new parents any day now. The kids will need something to keep themselves entertained so the parents can get their rest." Leo sat behind his desk. "Now, what is it you wanted to talk to me about? If it's Capone's Keys, I'm very pleased and excited about being a sponsor and am looking forward to the production. Imagine having such a historic and fascinating story right in our own backyard." He laced his hands on his desk.

"Umm, that's not why we're here," I said. "Connor and I want to talk to you about something else. How we're going to move forward with our relationship, especially after the girls arrive, and what you're expectations are regarding them, considering you'll be their biological grandfather."

"Ahh. It's an awkward situation, isn't it." Leo sounded like he understood, but did he?

"To say the least," said Connor. "We've looked into Florida law, so we know our rights. No one is currently aware you're Randi's biological father, and we want things to remain that way. You'll have no contact with the girls, no visitation, no rights. When, and if, the time comes that they need to know about you, we'll tell them who you are and how this came to be."

Silence spread across the desk like fog in a valley on a cold day. I tensed.

"I had my attorney look into this situation, too. He says we can amicably work something out so I can be part of their lives."

"I don't think so," said Connor.

"Is that your wish, too, Randi?" Leo gazed at me.

His heart and actions seemed to have softened since our first meeting at a Stitch In Time when he threatened to take my parents' property, and I hated to seem harsh. I had forgiven Leo for what he did to my mother, but now, I had to deal with the fallout where the twins were concerned. They would be born soon, and in a blink of an eye, they'd be grown. One day, they'd need to know.

"Yes, at least for now," I said.

Leo sat back. "Someday, I hope you'll reconsider. In the meantime, my attorney will continue to look into this matter. Grandparents can be of great benefit to parents and grandchildren. And grandchildren are very precious to grandparents." A glimmer of tears brimmed in Leo's eyes.

Connor and I rose and walked to the door.

"You forgot your gifts." Leo hurried around his desk, scooped up the packages, and handed them to us. "I'll see you at Capone's Keys next week. Looking forward to it," he said.

"So, how do you feel now that we've had the dreaded conversation?" Connor carried both gifts as we made our way to the car.

"Conflicted. I'm relieved Leo handled the conversation as calmly as he did, but confused that even after we expressed our legal rights and personal wishes, he still wants to figure out some way around them." I opened the car door and slipped inside.

Connor put the packages in the trunk then slid into the driver's seat. "I agree. On the one hand, he seems to have embraced the idea he'll be the grandfather of our twins. On the other, we know what he's capable of. Given his past, it's hard to know just what he's thinking."

"The good thing is, he didn't withdraw his sponsorship from Capone's Keys. That's a relief in and of itself."

Chapter 22

"There's a full house," said Connor, as we stood in the doorway of the studio and peeked around the corner at all the seated guests.

They'd paid big bucks to be part of the live reveal, and millions of others around the world waited online to view the long-buried mystery of Capone's Keys. The fact that we'd pulled off a fantastic event in such a short time that would raise an enormous amount of money for charity astounded me. And the best thing? My morning sickness was a thing of the past, and I could finally enjoy an event without having to excuse myself.

"Looks like everyone's in place. I guess we can get started." With my whole body tingling, I signaled our A/V folks and Rachel. She looked beautiful as she stepped to the podium.

"On behalf of A Stitch in Time in Boca Raton, Florida, welcome to one of the most exciting events the world has ever seen—the unveiling of Capone's Keys.

Tonight, for the first time, we will find out what Al Capone, the notorious Chicago gangster, hid in myriad safe deposit boxes throughout Florida in 1930 before he went to prison. Capone's niece said he hid one hundred million dollars in the boxes to be used for his retirement after he left prison. But because he had contracted syphilis, a debilitating disease left untreated, he couldn't remember where he'd hidden the lockbox.

"In 1948, Derick Eastway found a lockbox on a 55-acre island between Deerfield Beach and Boca Raton, Florida. The parcel, purchased by Al Capone in 1930 and referred to as Capone Island by locals, is now a Broward County Park named Deerfield Island Park. Before we get to the big reveal, please view a film that gives you a brief history of one of America's most notorious Prohibition gangsters. It will also include the backstory of his relationship to those whose names we could identify on the safe deposit keys—friends, foes, and simply acquaintances."

Rachel stepped aside, and the studio went black. On a large screen behind the stage, the film began with Capone's history of living in New York, his relationship with John Torrio, his moving to Chicago, and later Miami. We reenacted his procuring the safe deposit boxes, putting the keys into the lockbox, and burying it on Capone Island. And we reenacted Derick as an eleven-year-old boy finding the lockbox and taking it home.

A narrator told the story of how the lockbox came into my possession by way of Derick and Sheila Eastway. Then we introduced each person whose name we could decipher on the key tags and relayed their stories through their relatives either as a video or voice-over of the original remembrance. The lights came on at the end of the film, and Rachel returned to the podium.

"And now, for the great reveal performed by Reverend Lester Pearson, son of Dr. Homer Pearson whose father treated Al Capone for the flu and whose name was on one of the key tags."

Rachel stepped down, and our crew brought up a table and chair onto the stage. Two Boca Raton police officers wearing full uniforms and sidearms walked in and stood at attention behind the table. Kester came in carrying the lockbox and placed it on the table. Another detective entered with a safe deposit box and, likewise, set it on the table. Then, Reverend Lester Pearson walked in and sat. An overhead camera projected the rest of the dramatic results onto the screen.

The studio audience sat on the edge of their seats. Everyone, including the crew, held their breaths.

Kester opened the lockbox, lifted a safe deposit key with its dangling key tag, and handed it to Reverend Pearson. The pastor stuck the key into the safe deposit vault and turned it. He then removed the gray safe deposit box inside. Just as he was about to lift the lid, the studio doors burst open, and three suited men rushed in.

"FBI," they yelled in unison, each holding IDs above their heads.

Everyone gasped. Murmurings spread through the guests like the wave at a football game. Kester grabbed the gray box off the table and clutched it. The two Boca officers moved next to Kester, hands on their guns.

"I'm sorry, folks, but we'll need to take the safe deposit box." The lead FBI agent stepped forward.

Connor and I looked at each other, then made our way to the front of the studio.

"What's the meaning of this? I'm Connor Romero. My wife, Randi, owns the studio, and this is her event."

All eyes were on Connor.

"You the CID Special Agent?"

"Yes."

"Then you'll understand what we're doing and why. Please hand over the box." The agent extended his hand toward Kester, who tightly gripped the box, not moving.

I could see the guests' heads swiveling back and forth between the FBI agents, Connor, and Kester.

"What?" I said, stepping between the agent and Kester. "You can't do that. This is a private event." Was the agent going to quarrel with an arguably very pregnant woman?

"As representatives of the Federal Government, ma'am, yes we can. Curtis Canfield, the lab technician who ran tests on the keys, contacted us by obligation because he found a partial fingerprint he believed belonged to Al Capone on one of the key tags."

Everyone inhaled loudly, including me.

"Curtis never told us," I said.

"He wasn't allowed to, ma'am, or we would have arrested him. I'm sorry the timing worked out as it did, and we barged in on your event, but it took us a while to run a thorough analysis and comparison at the FBI lab. We just got confirming results yesterday. The print matches the index finger of Al Capone. Therefore, whatever is in the safe deposit box belongs to the federal government until cleared of ill-gotten gains. That means until we verify that whatever is in the box wasn't acquired through Capone's brothels, speakeasies, and illegal liquor sales, all assets will remain in federal custody."

Connor looked at me. "Honey, you knew this was always a possibility."

"You mean we'll never know what Capone put in the boxes?" I gazed at Connor, then at the agent.

"I'm sorry, ma'am, but we must take the box." The agent stepped toward Kester.

Connor nodded to Kester, who reluctantly handed the metal container to the agent.

We all stood there bewildered, frustrated, red-faced as the agents left. I wondered how the event played out across the internet. Would the debacle affect our customers, our reputation, our revenues?

"Wasn't that exciting, ladies and gentlemen?" said Rachel, returning to the podium and trying to turn an embarrassing situation into something positive. "Just like the vault in the Lexington hotel back in 1989, we'll never know what Al Capone placed in the safe deposit boxes. But we do know he put something in them under the names of individuals from whom we've just seen and heard, individuals who played a crucial role in the gangster's life.

"From a Stitch in Time in Boca Raton, Florida, we want to thank everyone in attendance and online for joining us. For those attending in the studio, please join us in the upholstery shop for refreshments. And don't forget to say hello to our special guests—those whose names are on the key tags."

As guests moved through the back studio doors toward the upholstery shop, I caught up with Reverend Pearson.

"I'm so sorry, Reverend Pearson. We had no idea this would happen." I didn't know what else to say to the man that may have just lost hundreds of thousands of dollars.

"It's all God's anyway, Randi. No matter what or how much was in the box, I can't take it with me." He shook hands with Connor and me and moved toward the shop.

"What an exciting ending," said Mrs. Jamieson. "You couldn't top that if you tried."

"You're not disappointed Reverend Pearson wasn't allowed to open the safe deposit box and let us know what was inside?" I stood next to Connor, believing the event was nothing short of a disaster.

"Heavens no, Randi! This was far more intriguing. Now, we'll forever wonder. But the best part is that we know the story of the safe deposit keys and lockbox is true. Capone did bury the box on the island. What a marvelous tale. Too bad Mr. Eastway wasn't here to see this." She hugged me and then made her way to the shop for refreshments.

"A fascinating event," said Leo Barlos. "Can't thank you enough for allowing me to be a sponsor. People will be talking about this for decades. By the way, how are you feeling?" He gazed down at my tummy.

I took a deep breath. I could pop at any minute. "As good as can be expected."

"Great," he said, placing a kiss on my cheek before excusing himself and following the crowd to the shop.

Connor and I stared at each other in astonishment. Had we made the right decision to exclude Leo from the twins' lives?

~

I pressed the code on the studio door to lock it tight, then Connor and I walked to the car, arms around each other. As we did, Kester approached.

"That was quite the event," he said.

"It certainly was. And while everyone we talked to found the ending quite exciting, after all I went through, I'm disappointed we weren't able to know once and for all what Capone put inside the boxes." I gazed at him, my eyes and mouth droopy sad.

"Then there's something you need to see." Kester reached into his jacket pocket and pulled something out. He stretched it between his fingers.

"What's this?" I asked, turning on my cell's flashlight and moving closer to see what he held in the waning light. "Why, that's a thousand-dollar bill! Where in the world did you get it?" I asked.

"Randi, that's not any one thousand dollar bill," said Connor, his voice infused with awe. "That's a 1928 thousand dollar Gold Certificate. See the gold seal on the left and the space on the right?" He pointed to the blank area. "Some people think the space was a mistake made at the mint, but the bill was designed that way. The space authenticates the bill."

"The government printed only 28,800 gold certificates in 1928, and today there are only a few hundred in existence," said Kester. "In today's market, a bill like this in good condition is worth about $3,000. The value jumps up to $10,000 for a bill in very fine condition and $18,000 for a bill in extremely very fine condition. For an uncirculated bill, the value hits $38,500. This bill would go somewhere between the last two values."

Connor and I glared at him wide-eyed.

"How'd you know that?" I asked.

"Conducted a little research on the internet while everyone else was partying down." Kester gave us a smug smile.

"But where did you get the bill?" I asked. Then, as though a bolt of lightning struck me, I realized where it came from. "You took it out of the safe deposit box!"

"It fell out," Kester corrected.

"So, Al Capone really did put millions of dollars in the boxes."

"Seems so," said Kester. "I've got to turn this back into the FBI, but I wanted you to see it first."

I took photos of the front and back of the bill. I'd frame both and hang them on my office wall.

"You know you're the best, don't you?" I kissed Kester on the cheek and gave him a hug.

"Saying that with your husband standing next to you is quite the compliment," he said. "Well, until next time, Mr. and Mrs. Romero. No, wait! I don't want a next time." Kester turned and waved his hand in the air as he walked away.

Connor and I broke into laughter. We knew somewhere down the road there'd be a next time.

Chapter 23

"You know this is the last of your capers and event, at least for a while." Connor sat on the edge of our bed, held my hands, and gazed lovingly at me.

"I know, but just look at all the good we did—finding murderers, arsons, and thieves."

"You forgot to mention that in these adventures, you've been kidnapped, sprayed with insecticide, and almost lost your life and that of the girls by drowning in the Intracoastal. And that doesn't include what happened earlier to Leslie and others."

"Well, none of this would have happened if you'd been partnering with me." I gave him one of my pouts.

"You mean like working together in an investigation firm?"

"Would that be so bad? You've developed a strong reputation for finding the truth in the Army, and so have I as a civilian. Brooks and Romero Investigations has a nice ring to it. Don't you think?" I looked at Connor and smiled.

"Romero and Brooks has a more official ring to it. After all, I'm the one with the credentials." Connor winked and gave me his sexy grin.

"Yeah, but I'm the one with the higher profile, now that millions of viewers have watched Capone's Keys." I put my arms around Connor's neck and pulled him close. "You can't deny this." I gave him a passionate kiss.

"That you've got the hottest lips around?" he asked. "I'd never deny that." He fused his soft lips to mine.

"Looks like you've got a knack for this, too, Mr. Romero. See what I mean about us being good together."

"In so many more ways than one." Connor lifted the covers and slipped into bed.

"I still like Brooks and Romero." I watched the sheet rise and fall as Connor's clothes came off one by one and dropped to the floor.

"And I still like Romero and Brooks." Connor unbuttoned my PJs and helped them off.

"So, how will we decide?" Our naked bodies melded together as close as my pumpkin belly would allow.

"Let's sleep on it," said Connor. "I'm sure we can come to some sort of compromise. Maybe we can consider Pauline Kincade's request for us to look into her brother's questionable suicide as our first case."

"Great idea! Pauline and Archie would be thrilled." I turned onto my left side. Connor wrapped his arms snuggly around me, molding himself to my back.

Just then, my body shuddered, and a loud groan echoed through the bedroom as a sharp contraction gripped me.

Sally J. Ling

NOTE TO THE READER

Thank you for reading *Capone's Keys,* the fourth book in A Randi Brooks Mystery series. I hope you enjoyed it. As reviews are important to every author, please take time to leave a review at Amazon.com.

The fifth book in this series is entitled *Half Gone.*

Half Gone

Randi wasn't looking for a new client, but when Archie talks her into speaking with a woman whose twin brother died under questionable circumstances, she decides to enlist Connor's aid in looking into the case.

Official reports from Miami cite the death as suicide, but further investigation by the newly formed team of Brooks and Romero finds missing reports, problematic crime scene practices, and evidence that proves otherwise.

They want authorities to take a second look at the case, yet their search for truth has landed them directly in someone's crosshairs. Despite the danger, Brooks and Romero are determined to reopen the twenty-year-old case others are convinced should remain closed.

ABOUT THE AUTHOR

Sally J. Ling, Florida's History Detective, is an author, speaker, and historian. She writes historical nonfiction, specializing in obscure, unusual, or little-known stories of Florida history and mysteries with a Florida connection.

As a special correspondent, Sally wrote for the *Sun-Sentinel* newspaper for four years and was a contributing journalist for several South Florida magazines.

Based upon her knowledge as well as excerpts from her books, Sally has appeared in three feature-length TV documentaries—"Gangsters," the National Geographic Channel; "The Secret Weapon that Won World War II," and "Prohibition and the South Florida Connection," WLRN, Miami. She served as associate producer on the latter production. She has also appeared in and served as a production consultant for several short documentaries on South Florida history produced by WLRN, Miami.

Sally has been a repeat guest on South Florida PBS TV and radio stations, guest presenter at the Lifelong Learning Society at Florida Atlantic University, and guest speaker at numerous historical societies, libraries, organizations, and schools.

Sally lives with her husband, Chuck, in South Florida.

For information on Sally's current projects, or to become a "Preferred Reader" and receive notices on upcoming books. please visit her website at:

sallyjling.com

To engage Sally as a speaker, or to send her an email, contact her at:

info@sallyjling.com

Sally's books include:

Fiction

- *Frayed Ends: A Randi Brooks Mystery (Book 1)*
- *Uncovered: A Randi Brooks Mystery (Book 2)*
- *Orchid Fever: A Randi Brooks Mystery (Book 3)*
- *Capone's Keys: A Randi Brooks Mystery (Book 4)*
- *Women of the Ring*
- *Who Killed Leno and Louise?*
- *The Cloak: A Shea Baker Mystery (Book 1)*
- *The Spear of Destiny: A Shea Baker Mystery (Book 2)*
- *The Twelfth Stone: A Shea Baker Mystery (Book 3)*
- *The Tree and the Carpenter*
- *Spies, Root Beer and Alligators: Phillip's Great Adventures (Children's Novel)*

Nonfiction
- *Deerfield Beach: The Land and Its People*
- *Al Capone's Miami: Paradise or Purgatory?*
- *Out of Mind, Out of Sight: A Revealing History of the Florida State Hospital at Chattahoochee and Mental Health Care in Florida*
- *Sailin' on the Stranahan (commissioned coffee table book)*
- *Run the Rum In: South Florida during Prohibition*
- *Small Town, Big Secrets: Inside the Boca Raton Army Airfield during World War II (First and Second editions)*
- *A History of Boca Raton*
- *Fund Raising With Golf*

Made in the USA
Middletown, DE
23 April 2023

29249983R00133